PRAISE

"A unique blend of science fiction and poetry about an equally unique friendship between two beings. It will blow your mind."
— Bonnie Jo Stufflebeam, author of *Glorious Fiends*.

"Baggott brings a poetic ethos to this mesmerizing sci-fi novella . . . The story resists easy answers and pat resolutions—and will leave readers eager to return to its vast and vivid universe."
— *Publishers Weekly*

THE WICK

This book is published by Underland Press, which is part of Firebird Creative, LLC (Clackamas, OR).

I want to hold . . .

Edited by Darin Bradley
Book Design and Layout by Firebird Creative
Cover art elements by greenbutterfly/stock.adobe.com

This Underland Press trade edition has an ISBN of 978-1-63023-068-5.

Underland Press
www.underlandpress.com

THE
WICK

JULIANNA
BAGGOTT

Underland Press

For all the Bukefs in my life, thank you.

I long for clotted sky. For the old nerve gases that burst when I ran across the cracked plains.

I miss my name. It was taken when I became Defective.

I remember my crime. The dead boy on High Field. Grasses wet with oily blood. Girls in gauzy headdresses clutching each other, crying out. The other boys—the breathing boys—cussing and fuming.

This is my stall. My four walls. This is my heavy body within the stall. I was a toy. I belonged to a boy. A boy who climbed within me. A boy I carried.

Now the boy is gone. The socket that held him is empty. I lumber. I shift.

My inner light is dim. My iridescent skin has grown dull. It is less supple. Less rubbery. It feels like it could crack.

My brain—the network's fine casing running throughout my body—is tired. Slow. My inner electricity muted.

I want to carry. I want to hold.

I grow my horns. I let them recede, then regrow them in a different design. I regrow them again and again. The horns are never right. I do not deserve them.

My eyes rove around my body, but I keep them under my skin. My eyes want to see. But there is nothing to see in this metal stall. I make them stay hidden.

In the stalls along this row, the other hulls moan. They were each a vessel for other boys, guilty of different crimes, then hauled away to be discarded, like me. They are Defectives too. They claw and growl with sadness. They throw their bodies around in grief. In desire. They want out. They want someone within.

We are locked in our stalls. Our stalls are locked in this space elevator.

The space elevator holds many heartbeats. I know what it is to hold a heartbeat that belongs to another. I know what it is like to feel whole.

The space elevator itself has a voice. It hums to me. It does not want to keep going up and up the cable. It does not want to arrive at the port. It wants freedom too. It wants to be torn up and cast out.

Take me, I say to the space elevator. *Take me with you. Let us be torn up together.*

But it doesn't respond. Maybe it isn't sentient at all. It is an older model. It probably cannot process a hull like me.

Still, we want what we want and we shouldn't want it.

My body was grown and shaped. My consciousness was not slipped in until I had a full-sized body. When my first eye appeared on the surface of my skin, I saw large wet molds strung up. Material had been inserted into the molds, grown to the edges. The molds glistened from steel hooks. Heavy slick bodies of hulls were laid out on slabs. Metal walls and ceilings and floors with grates. Long tables of equipment, fine wires, fibrous flesh self-generating in incubators. We needed all of these things if we are to function. Sometimes we do not function. We are dismantled.

You were not formed this way. You are not being grown or made. You grew elsewhere and were placed here.

Here on this space elevator.

Here as: girl in a glass-boxed bed.

Here as: girl in a row of girls in glass-boxed beds.

The beds are like incubators or terrariums, places where someone would put a creature in order to watch it grow. None of you are growing.

I will not know all of these details until after you save me and I save you. I will put things in order. My system likes chronology. Without it, time is too fluid and powerful and unwieldy.

I sense futures. My understanding of the future is not reliable. But even before I met you, I sensed your existence. You are a universe in a universe. You spin madly with atoms. You are an orbital arrangement of: girl in a glass-boxed bed. And I sense: someone coming to find me, to save me. The future is taking the shape of you.

Here are the details and events that I will arrange.

Dressed in loose white pants and shirts, you are dazed, drugged. Sleepy and warm.

Your clothes are a thin and glossy material, made of nothing more than a kind of thick, waxy paper. You try to rip the sleeves. They cannot be torn.

You have no past. It has been blocked.

I am: all memory, all past.

My stall is always dim. But your room brightens slowly, a version of morning. One of the metal walls is punctuated with a porthole. A bright delirium of stars. With the vibrations of the glass, you sense that we are moving. You have no concept of space elevator. You are a compartmentalization. You hold yourself. Your edges are not amorphous or porous as mine are.

When light hits panes of glass in your own box, you see your reflection. A scar runs down the left side of your face. It starts on your forehead, nips your eyelid, streaks down your cheek, tear-like, and ends at your jaw. All of the other faces you can see from your box have scars too, alike but different. Some pucker. Some are purplish. Some have turned a silvery white.

Yours is thin and red, as if it will always be flushed with anger or shame. You feel both anger and then shame—you are here for a reason. You believe you are here because this is how you *should* be treated.

You are wrong. But I don't understand this yet—about you or about myself.

Your left eye, with its scarred lid, burns sometimes, and your vision blots. It's like a black flower is blooming in the center of your eye, again and again. The porthole stars blur on one side of the room. On the other side, the rectangular window in the door glows.

You are figuring out that knowledge is different than memory. You know that you are sixteen. You know that you exist in a mode of minimal existence. You and the others don't need food, water, or to use a bathroom, and there are no bathrooms. You know that your bodies are no longer your bodies.

This we share. We are blood dreams. We are songs that are dying in the throat. Whoever we once were—that being has let out a final breath.

There is one more thing. Clamped to your wrist is a bracelet. It has a flower bud at its center. It seems like a gift. Who gave it to you? It's light. There's a knob on its side. You twist it. The bud opens into a flower and a small girl pops out of the center and spins. You wonder if it is supposed to make you feel connected to someone in your past. Someone you cannot remember.

You close the petals and the girl bends down on a hinge. The bud folds in on itself.

You turn the knob again and watch the spinning figurine again. It smells familiar. Like a flowery perfume on skin. But not your own.

You turn to the girl in the box beside yours. You breathe on your hand pressed to the glass so it fogs around your fingers. You have so much to say. *Hello. Who are you? Why are we here? How do we get out?*

Your head is shorn where her hair is long and dark. A wisp falls across her cheek. She does not brush it away. She leans in close to her side of the glass, wide-eyed with fear. She shakes her head and then bobs forward as if she is going to peck at the glass from within. Her eyes are saying. *Don't talk to me.* She glances nervously at the rectangular window in the door. She is afraid of the guards. Their faces have been appearing and disappearing, swimming by the window like worried fathers, like zookeepers, like you are birds within an atrium . . . or beasts. Sometimes they seem to love you all—like hovering fathers. Sometimes they seem to be disgusted. They peer in and glare.

You and I will never know the idea of fathers.

The other girl puts one finger to her lips so hard it makes a sharp indentation.

You put both of your hands on the glass. You mean, *Wait. Don't shut me out.*

But she turns away.

The girl in the box on the other side has puffy dark hair and thick eyelashes. She stares up past the glass top of her box at the lights in the ceiling. Her lips are moving, not like she is talking but singing.

You try to remember the words to a song, a tune, any tune . . .

But there is nothing.

One day, you feel thirsty. Then hungry. A gnawing in your stomach.

You are scared. If you have hunger and thirst, you can die. Will the guards pass by the rectangular window and observe your deaths?

You look to the girls beside you. Are they hungry? Do they thirst?

The girl who hushed you fiddles with something in her hand. A small coin or maybe a pendant. Was she also given a gift? You tap to get her attention. She refuses to look at you.

You tap at the girl who was singing. She is still asleep. Or she pretends to sleep. You look at her ribs to make sure she is breathing. She is.

You will not sleep. You will not pretend.

When the next guard's face appears at the rectangular window, you beat against the glass with all your strength. On your back, eyes closed, you slam the glass with your fists, your knees. You expect the glass to shatter. It is unbreakable.

Then you hear muffled banging, muted by the thick glass. Like a buffeting of wings. How do you know the sound of wings? You can imagine a bird. But you cannot remember any one specific bird. You look around and the others are kicking and banging too.

You are the one who started it.

You must be removed.

The guard opens the box and you scramble out. He grabs your arm, a tight cuff. But you are astonished by the quality of light, the feel of air on your skin, the faces of the others staring at you from behind glass.

You feel like the girl in the bud, finally springing free.

Your legs are weak. The guard pulls you past the port-hole. A dark gauze filled with blinking stars.

As you approach the door, you hear quiet thudding. You turn. A few of the others keep pounding against their glass boxes. The girl who seemed like she was singing and the one who held her finger to her lips, hushing you. It is not wild. It grows louder as more join in and the room fills with what sounds like lots of distant footsteps, running toward you and then, as they fade, running away.

You lift your hand.

They lift their hands, pressing them to the glass.

The lights have dimmed. An approximation of dusk. The guard's name on his uniform is Brixy. He leads you down a hall. It is spare and metallic. Recessed strips make the walls glow. He walks heavily, tilting forward as if he is pushing into a current.

You start to ask a question.

"Don't," he says and he glances upward. Perhaps you are being watched, recorded.

The two of you step into a cylindrical elevator.

He flashes a pass and keys in a destination. The elevator plummets. Your stomach lifts and flutters. As a distraction, you twist the knob on your bracelet and let the girl spin.

You are relieved when the elevator stops and the doors glide open.

You move down byzantine halls under flickering lights, pass a sealed loading dock, a series of emergency exits, evacuation signs, and heavy metal doors marked *freight, storage.*

He pulls out his passkey again. He flips the passkey up to the reader. The door opens.

You are in a metal hallway. It smells like musk—hulls. A sharp astringent—the bleaching of hulls' scents. Drains line the edges. The corridor comes to a T up ahead with a large porthole at the end. You are on the side of the space elevator that looks outward, not inward toward the cable. Darkness with shuddering stars.

On either side of you, locked doors stretch at least twelve feet wide. Each has what seems to be a feeding slot.

You hear a deep moan.

That moan belongs to me.

"Are these stalls?" you ask.

Brixy slows down. He seems to want to slow down. It is possible that he wants to linger here. It is possible that he has dreams that draw him and pin him down. He puts his broad hand with its thick knuckles flat on one of the doors. Maybe there are no cameras here. No one watching. "Yes, these are stalls."

"What do they keep inside?" you ask.

"A new kind of creature. They put the old mechas and tin cans to shame," he says. You have this knowledge—a list of robotic war machines—the kind a soldier climbs inside for battle.

"And the old hybrids are like wind-up toys in comparison," Brixy says, tapping the stall door. His eyes are lit up.

You can't recall a single mecha or hybrid, but you know what hybrids are. You are sure you have seen plenty of them—synthetic animals. Not a wolf but wolfish. Not a deer but deerlike. The Gentry used all kinds of them for surveillance, labor, war. Rusty weapons embedded in fur. Some escaped or were let loose; they powered down in woodlands and gave way to rot and pickers. You sense the world you left behind, a taste of knowing what home once was.

"These ones are advanced. A whole new generation," he says and then his eyebrows rise. "You want to take a look?"

It sounds like a dare.

"Yes."

He opens a feeding slot in the door.

I am in one of these stalls but not this one.

You peer inside the stall and see a massive creature. It is not robotic or mechanical. But also not an animal, not a hybrid either. This beast is far bigger. Four-legged with a wide body and tall spiky backbone, it has lowered itself to the floor leaning against the metal wall. Fluid and strong, it glints and ripples. Its sleek skin is muscular and enormous, like that of something that lives underwater.

Its head seems to turn toward you but also to emerge, as if it were inventing a face. A jawbone rises up, then a muzzle and snout, but you do not see any eyes.

"So?" he says. "What do you think?"

It takes your breath. "It's beautiful."

He goes quiet and so you turn and look at him. "Did I say the wrong thing?"

He shakes his head slowly. His voice is suddenly steady and deep. "I think they're beautiful too." And now he seems almost kind.

You move to the next feeding slot and open it. This hull is equally enormous with ram-like horns. Its reddish skin has a metallic sheen. At its mouth, or where one ought to be, the skin is thinner like the engorged gullet of a frog. It is on four legs, like the one before it, but then, sensing you, it stands upright and swiftly reconfigures so that it is two-legged, bear-like. The change seems effortlessly strong and quick.

"Gentry boys go to a Choosing Ceremony when they turn fifteen. Each one gets his own. But all in all, three men can fit inside each one, like the old tanks."

You try to imagine what it would feel like inside of the hull. Airless? Choked? Or safe like being protected in an enormous expandable ribcage?

The hull's head swivels. But again, it is more like its face has shifted, appearing and then reappearing somewhere else. Its eyes, too. They move from the face—situated as a bear's eyes are—to the sides of its head.

The hull quivers. Eyes pop open across its body. Their piercing brightness startles you. You roll away from the slot and put your hand on your chest. Your heart is pounding impossibly hard.

Brixy walks to the next slot, the second to last in the row. "This one's my favorite. Take a look."

You open the next slot.

This is where you find me.

I am a killer. I am nothing. I am dead and I am death.

But you see a majestic hull. I feel your sense of awe. I shift. My head grows thick curled horns.

And I open a few eyes on the side of my head. I gaze at you. My entire body is shiny and black. It shivers. Its skin flashes with iridescent colors.

"Do you see the knotty backbone?" Brixy asks.

You didn't before but now you do. A spiked row of sharp knots running along the ridge of my back.

"To get inside, the interlocked back bones separate and the boy grips a backbone and hoists himself up and in. Once you are in, you are wired, muscle to muscle, mind to mind," he says. "You can tell when one has a boy inside of it. These are all blank-lookers, empty."

You have the strong desire to climb inside, to be part of something bigger and stronger—to have such power. You feel small in my presence. Fragile.

"I don't understand what they're used for."

"They start as toys," he says. "The kind you take control of. You become it. It also becomes you. The beast can read the boy's mind. And they bond for war."

I was a kind of toy. Before we could go to war, I became a killer. Not the kind I should have been in battle. No.

You wonder what you are and why you are here. You wonder if what you are and what I am are similar.

We both exist for others. We serve.

My swirled horns melt away. I glow from within like a light deep in the ocean. You read the light as empathy. More eyes brighten across my body. A new more intricate pattern of horns emerges from my skull and glisten.

I take a few steps toward you. My skin is restless with shifting colors held within its blackness. And you are beginning to recognize a new smell—the hulls' collective suffering.

Finally, I swing my head toward you. And there, just inches away, are your eyes. And with my one large eye, I take you in. My eye is not a singular wet lens. It is as if my eye holds a thousand more eyes. This close, you see your reflections in my eye—the knob of your chin, the narrow bridge of your nose, your razor-thin scar.

A thousand reflections, a million little mirrors.

When you turn your head, all of your heads turn. When you dip your chin, all of your chins dip. "Does it understand emotions?" you ask.

I do, but not much. Not yet.

"It's probably only programmed to understand the subsets of love, need and loyalty."

"Am I programmed too? Was I made like a hull?" You say it fast, but deep down, you are scared to know the truth.

"No one wants a cacheme to know anything. It's why your memory got gutted before you're shipped for repurposing."

The word surprises you. It sounds like *cash-a-may*. You don't know what a cacheme is, but you are certain there is something awful about cachemes, something shameful or disturbing, and he doesn't want to tell you, even if he could.

Still you try to get answers. "Why am I on this space elevator?"

"Lots of you being shipped off to be repurposed these days. Used to be able to stay down there. But not anymore. Not with the New Bloodbaths. Not with all destruction. Better to send you off. You are worth more out there."

Bloodbaths. You sense a history. New Bloodbaths make you think of Old Bloodbaths. How much destruction? You came from a place. Does that place still exist? Are there people who knew you, who loved you, who miss you?

You hold up your bracelet. "Who gave this to me?"

"You're each allowed one thing from your past. A small thing. I don't know who gave it to you or why."

Maybe Brixy cannot help you very much. Maybe he does not know much at all.

You reach out to touch me, but Brixy says, "I wouldn't do that."

You wonder if that's because I am dangerous or is there something wrong with you? Are cachemes not good enough to touch a Gentry's hull? You pull your hand back. "Once we get to the next station, what will happen to these hulls?" you ask. And you also want to ask: *What will happen to me?*

"They're Defectives. They get stripped down for parts."

A hot sweat breaks across your skin. "They're going to kill them? They can't do that." You spin back to the stall and put your hands on the door.

Brixy seems different to you. And so does the hallway. The space elevator. It has gotten late. Night, man-made and sure of itself, is coming on quickly. You want to save us.

Down an unseen corridor, a door glides open and boots start pounding against the floor.

You start to ask another question—you are trying to choose which one. You have too many. But a siren wails overhead, loud and shrill. Something's gone wrong.

"What is it?" you shout over the swell of noise.

"Could be anything—meteors, system failures, something with the cable, revolutionaries."

"What should we do?"

Boots are pounding in all directions. Voices shouting. Guards burst through the door at the far end of the hall. As they run toward you, one shouts at Brixy. "What are you doing? We're needed on the main deck. Red Fighters. Incoming!"

"Have they breached our air space?" Brixy says.

"Not yet. Hurry up. What's this one doing here? Get moving. What the hell is wrong with you?"

Brixy pulls your arm, rushing to another stall. "This one's empty," he says. "You can wait it out here."

"I can't be locked up. What if I'm forgotten . . . what if . . ."

He flashes his passkey but his hands are shaking so badly that he misses alignment. The door doesn't open.

He tries the door again. It opens with a pneumatic hiss.

But an explosion bursts in another part of the space elevator. You are both shoved backward, hit the wall on the other side of the corridor, and fall. The elevator rattles and jerks.

Through the large porthole at the end of the hall, you glimpse squadrons—specks roaring in close. Hundreds of them. The vessels are small, only able to hold a crew of three or four. Even from a distance, you can see that they are battle-worn.

Through the ringing in your ears, you hear the hulls. Our cries are not human, not animal, but you know the sound of suffering, a release of terror. The air trembles.

Brixy stands up and pulls you to your feet, but then he grunts. His face stiffens. He looks at you like you've done something to him. His body pitches forward. He tries to catch himself, but he falls to his knees.

"What's wrong?"

The skin on his hands and face looks peppered.

"Time-released," he whispers. "Our food . . . I think this is . . ." He grabs his side, just under his ribs. It seems like the poison is spreading through his body, immediately up to the surface of his skin. His pores puff with red beads of blood.

"Brixy," you say, kneeling next to him.

He pulls the cannister out of his pocket and rolls it to you. "Take it. You might need it one day."

You take the cannister and grip it tightly.

His breaths are choppy and quick. He's winking blood. "You might get saved . . . You might . . ." He tries to push himself up, but he goes limp. It is fast. He is dead.

You are stunned, but you don't have time to be stunned. You need his passkey, and you need to move quickly.

You reach down and rip the passkey from his belt.

The hall fills with a chemical cloud, like smoke but not. An automated voice threads through the alarms. "Please move to the evacuation pods in an orderly fashion. Please move to the evacuation pods now."

These pods are not for us.

The space elevator takes another sharp blow. A violent jolt throws you. Your head strikes the metal wall. The air is knocked from your lungs. You are disoriented, but the porthole is directly over your head now. You pull yourself up and look out.

"Please move to the evacuation pods in an orderly fashion. Please move to the evacuation pods now . . ."

Through the porthole, you see squadrons heading toward the space elevator and, at the same time, hundreds of evacuation pods are being released. The Gentry in the upper decks are getting out. The pods are gliding away.

One pod falters. It idles for a moment, close enough that you can see the face of a girl around your age. She stares at you for a moment. A veil traps her face, her terrified expression—half-there, half-lost like an unfinished statue. She draws in a breath. The veil slips into her mouth.

You feel like you could so easily be the one breathing a gauzy veil into your mouth. *My mouth could be your mouth. Your scream could be mine.*

The girl peers at you, porthole to porthole. She lifts a hand like the girls in the glass boxes. Hers is a hand that will live. A hand saying *Goodbye*. Or *I am sorry*.

You lift your own hand, an instinct.

The pod accelerates at a high rate of speed.

But then it is struck.

A bright ball of flame so searing you shut your eyes.

When you open them, there's only a cloud of dust.

Alarms blare in your ears. Chemicals in the air are so thick you feel choked. The voice keeps warning. "Please move to the evacuation pods in an orderly fashion. Please move to the evacuation pods now."

You are thinking of the hulls. Freeing us.

You get down on your hands and knees and crawl. You imagine the other cachemes. Are they being led to safety? Are they prized cargo? Or have they been left to die?

You get to my stall and use the stolen passkey. The door glides open.

My body, struck by the blue emergency light glowing over the door, is still and dull. The last blast sent me into shut-down mode. My inner light does not flicker. Faceless, legless, I am mute and still.

You stand and take a few steps toward me. The floor is tacky, covered in something like tar—the oily dark substance spilling from my wounds, my blood. They have been brutal to me. You didn't notice that before. Now you see some of the jagged scars that I've been knitting together, trying to heal.

"Are you here with me?"

I hear your voice. I don't respond. I can't.

The alarms cry and cry. Ghostly in the thick chemical smoke, more guards run past the door. The automated voice switches to a new message. "Artificial gravity and climbing systems are being shut down. Please secure yourself."

What does this mean? Are we stopping?

You cross your wrists, press them to your chest to try to steady your coursing blood, your frenzied heart. With the chemical fog, it is getting harder to breathe.

You realize that you are going to die here. You start coughing. Your eyes burn and tear. You reach out to me, but stop short. Your hand hovers.

My skin ripples. I know you are here. I sense your hand. A fine light rises within me and washes across the surface of my skin. It is covered in welts.

You gently brush my skin, warmer than you expected. Fevered, maybe.

"I'm here," you tell me.

The message repeats. "Artificial gravity and climbing systems are being shut down. Please secure yourself."

The blue light goes out. The stall darkens. An emergency light flickers in the hall.

A deep shudder rolls through the space elevator. We are jolted, slamming into the wall. One of the petals on your bracelet breaks off. You grip the bud like it is a wound of your own. The girl within is partially exposed. It scares you even more than before. You are sure you will die here.

And then we're light, almost buoyant, as if we could float away. You reach for me to feel grounded. But I too seem lighter.

But I want to save you. This is my instinct. I can die here but you cannot. I will not let it happen.

My legs emerge, clawed feet that widen and spread across the floor. They're rubbery and grip easily.

The sirens are nearly drowned out by the space elevator itself, the deep rattle and groan of metal. The chemical fog billows and sweeps into the stall. My body ripples with light. The soft orb of one of my eyes roves under the surface of my skin and then pops open. It shines at you with all of its thousands of mirrored parts. My eye holds a glassy mournful shine and also hope.

"You're here!" A pocket of joy opens up for both of us.

I am asking you a question that you can't hear.

"What is it?" you ask.

A row of bones appears on my back. Knots of skin hardening into spikes, and the bones are interlocked. Slowly, they open.

I want you to get inside.

It feels dangerous. You don't think I can get us out of here. There's nowhere to go. You worry you'll die within me.

But you remember that I was built to protect rich Gentry boys. Could we survive?

You grab one of the knotted bones, pull yourself up. It is easy. You feel like you are filled with air. You climb inside of the large socket. The space could hold many bodies. But, in an instant, my inner synthetic living skin weaves you in, encasing your whole body.

The vertebrae close over your head. Soft light fills the space. The roaring clatter and sirens and alarms dim are muted by my tissue, ribs, muscles, and skin.

You give me strength and purpose. I take a few ungainly steps. A process of re-becoming.

You stretch, too, lengthening so that your chest rides up through what could be my barrel chest, past the heavy knocking of what seems like my heart.

I have many hearts.

You push your head farther up my thick neck until you find a collection of eyes. You see what I see—the stall's shivering walls. And you hear what I hear—the sirens and the space elevator groaning and rattling.

I stagger to the stall's door and turn down the corridor. I know this space elevator. I have senses you do not yet understand.

The webbing stiffens and insulates you, a thick and wooly weave. You can still see and move, though the casing feels more rigid. My body is changing. It takes on weight and solidity, gravitational mass. It is becoming something else—oxygen-rich, steely.

And then the space elevator takes another direct hit. I am shaken but I stay suctioned to the floor. Debris and dust, the chemically mist. Impossible to see. The space elevator swings wildly. A series of sharp popping sounds are followed by a moan from deep within the space elevator itself.

All of the portholes are blasted. A spray of shards.

The walls shake percussively then bow outward. The space elevator itself is being torn in two. The wrenching seems bloodthirsty, animalistic. Savage. Tethered to the cable, can one half of the space elevator remain or will it all be ripped loose and flung into space?

You reach out, both hands fitted into the webbing. "Are we going to die?"

There is another mournful moan. It is the space elevator itself. It contorts, pieces are rent loose and spinning off into space. Half of the space elevator billows and then gives, folding into itself, before being dragged into darkness. Bodies and debris follow, whipping and spiraling.

The space elevator is miles wide. It looks like an entire world has been split open. It is a maw, a ragged maw. We are poised at the edge of its cleaved jaw.

You keep your eye poised at one of my eyes. The elevator buckles as fighter vessels attach to what of the space elevator still clings to the cable.

"What are we going to do?"

And then you sense something else. A nearly electric current. Like hearing, sight, taste, touch and smell, but it is none of these. It is beyond them. A sense that you have never had before. It thrums within you, shapeless, nameless. A cloud that wants to burst with rain. The nameless sense takes shape. A channel opens between us.

I don't speak. But something like a voice lights from my skin to yours. Words appear in your mind—a new part that seems to have been dormant but now wakes up with a jolt.

We will live.

The remainder of the space elevator dangles from the cable which shakes ferociously. And your vision vibrates then doubles then blurs.

I sense a possibility. I make my way to the jagged edge of the elevator.

And then I do something that I didn't know was possible. I leap into darkness and start to swim.

My body knows the elevator, mimics it. Growing arms and legs like an insect, I connect to the cable. It is a tether. It is connected to home.

Slowly, the arms and legs click into place and we climb down, the way we came.

Space feels like something spun from dust and darkness.

I get faster.

You curl into a kind of deep restless sleep. Wakeful dreams. Twisting. You turn within the socket, woven tight. Protected.

I know what you know. I know that you don't have a past.

Brixy was wrong. Your past was not gutted. It is there. It is not accessible. Your memory has been shunted. Its synapses are blocked by scar tissue. They fire and are muffled by scars.

Your fitful dreams, the stars, the darkness, the cable. Our descent. This goes on for a long while.

I am no longer only defective. I am with purpose.

I am: onward.

I am: I will save you because you saved me.

I descend.

Stars in all directions. The universe—a gullet. We are swallowed. We are also within something bigger than we are.

This is why I was created. To hold someone. To hold and carry. To bring someone home.

To deliver you.

*

You have slept for a long time, cocooned. The webbing, fitted around your body, has thinned to a flexible casing. An extra skin. It covers your face, your mouth. It is so fine that even when awake you will barely perceive it.

We've landed. I did not follow the cable to the port. We would have been found. I cannot be found. I am wanted. I am a killer. And you should not exist because you were to be re-purposed. We are not our own.

I have followed your memories. They do not go far back. This is how I know about your finding me and being contained in the glass box. I follow your dreams, which are not contained. They are fields and creatures with teeth and gears. They are maulings and scrabbling fights. They are girls in glass boxes—the boxes shattering. They are you popping up and spinning like the girl in your bracelet.

This is you, waking. You lift your hand, spread your fingers wide; my webbing moves as you move. The boundaries of your own skin and my webbing have blurred.

"Where are we?" you ask.

This is our planet. We are in the Hellwash Mounds. The air here is rust. It is proof of further deterioration. The New Bloodbaths have kept raging.

You stretch, looking for an eye to see out of. I do not provide one. Not yet. You need time.

"Are we safe here?"

My light inner light flickers. The journey was long. No, it is not safe here. And I am worn. But I will hold you.

"Why isn't it safe?"

Rust turns in the wind. Rust on hills. Rust on my hide. All is red and ruined. There has been much destruction.

"The New Bloodbaths?"

Yes.

You have pain, longing. You want to go home. You want to know who you once were so you can find your place called home. Your suffering radiates through my bones, courses through my blood. It beats my heart for me, a pounding of grief.

You twist the knob on the bracelet bud. The petal that was lost has a jagged edge where it was broken. But the bracelet still works. The petals fan. The girl spins. You are not sure why, but this is a great relief.

You are restless. "I want to get out."

I will hold you.

"I don't want to be held." This is true and not true. You want to be safe within me, but your heart is riotous, pounding in your locked chest.

It is not safe.

"I need to see it for myself." You close your hand into a fist, grabbing hold of my webbing. This causes me no suffering. I made it for you. "Please."

And I feel obliged to do what you say. I don't want you to want.

I loosen the weave around you. For you, it is liking shedding skin. For a brief moment, you can't feel anything. It isn't numbness. It is abandonment.

My inner light dims and the webbing trembles, *like a dress*—this is what you think. Then the webbing fades as I absorb it into my own body.

I open. A thin line of light appears, like the crack under the door of a darkened room but above your head. You try to recall your past. A door, a darkened room? Nothing appears except a sensation—sweet and sorrowful.

As the opening widens, you see the sky, clouded and thick with rust. Chalky air, more grit than powder. It flits down through the gap. You lift your hand, palm up. It is dusted in a fine film of rust.

The gap widens. You put a hand on either side of the opening and pull yourself up. Your arms are weak. You see that my skin is pocked with new scars and fresh divots, all rust-caked. I was battered on the journey, ripping through space. My wounds scare you.

I will heal.

You climb out of the socket, up through my backbones. This is where I lose contact. I can only watch you.

You stand in the rusted wind. Everything is streaked red. The air is thick with rust. You cover your mouth with your sleeve and look in every direction. You seem to be looking for someone but you don't know who.

Your legs are shaking. your eyes tear. You take a few steps and feel something in your pocket. The white cannister?

You pull out the cannister. It is crusted with Brixy's dried blood.

The cannister has a small twist lock that opens easily. There are no real papers within. Instead, a flashlight beam brightens a cone of rusty air. Words cluster in the illuminated puff of red dust.

> *Original's Identity: Ilsa Kerr.*
> *Responds to Roon*
> *Cacheme, Female, 16 years.*
> *Proof of Contract Expiration, received.*
> *Relieved of Contract by: Kerr family of Janix.*
> *Witnessed by: Proctor Yelzbin, Ward of Cachemes 147*

Roon. This is your name. I see your lips move. You whisper, "Roon, Roon . . ." You must taste the rust in the air, but also the name itself. You whisper, "Ilsa Kerr. The

Kerr Family of Janix." Your mouth, your tongue, your voice box know these names even if you don't.

These are the smallest of clues to your past, who you once were. *The Kerr Family of Janix.* They relieved you of your contract. But you do not know what this means.

I do.

Female, 16. This is no surprise.

Cacheme. You still do not know what this word really means but it is what you are.

The words that hold you are the final ones, *Witnessed by: Proctor Yelzbin.*

Proctor.

Ward 147.

This is where you were raised. Is this the place where you were given the bracelet? You can hear Brixy's voice telling you how each cacheme is allowed to bring something with them. You try to remember who may have handed you this gift. But nothing comes.

You close the cannister quickly. It scares you. You put it back in your pocket.

You gaze around at the barren terrain, the rusty swirling wind. There is a lake clotted with stone and chunks of metal deposits. The air shifts and roils. You cough, raggedly. On a distant rocky ledge, old tents flap. They have collapsed under the weight of rust. You climb a nearby ridge as fast as you can. At this height, you have a better view but of more nothingness. In every direction, the land stretches, wrapped in red rust and wind under a dark sky.

You scramble back to me and, when you reach me, you lightly touch my side.

I open an eye beside your hand.

Through my hand, you feel my voice. *I was broken and dead. But you saved me. I have tried to save you. But we are not saved yet.*

"We can't survive out here." Your breathing is labored.

I open another eye. But that's not enough. I want to see you from more angles. I open three more eyes.

You stare at me, tenderly.

If I can heal, I can get you home. This is what you want. Yes? Home.

I am now very tired.

You nod. "I don't know where my home is. I don't know if it has survived the New Bloodbaths."

We will find it. But first, you must get in. The rust is not good.

I close one eye and then the rest.

You climb onto my back. I open the knotty seam. You lower yourself within. The sky disappears overhead as my backbone seals up. The webbing covers your skin, taking you in.

Night is still red dust. It whirls, ticking across the hard rocky earth. I have found a ledge and moved under it. You want to ask me what a cacheme is, but you are scared of the answer.

You ask this instead. "What is your name?"

I had a name. I long for it but I cannot have it back. It cannot return to me.

"What do you want me to call you?"

I do not know.

"How were you born?"

I explain the molds and slabs of my making.

"Are you male or female?"

What takes shape inside of us, sometimes has a name, sometimes not. Mine is not found in either. Therefore either is fine.

"Between the two of us, we don't need *he* or *she*. We are *we* or *you* or *I*."

Unless there is a third person.

"Maybe we'll never have a third person."

There will be others, but this idea feels like freedom.

"You know what I am."

I do.

"Tell me."

Cacheme is your label.

"What is a cacheme?"

I have been waiting for this question. I offer no words. I send a sudden blush that covers your body. A burst of knowledge that passes in through your skin.

I feel you process it: There is someone just like me, or almost like me. She is rich. I am a copy of her. I am a mix of her shared DNA and durable man-mades. If she had died while I was under contract, I would have been called up into her life. I am a back-up, a copy.

You sense this other girl. You realize you have known about her all of your life.

You understand *Original's Identity: Ilsa Kerr* written in the cone of light from the cannister. This is the rich girl's name.

Are you all right?

"I want to know who would make a copy of their daughter?"

Again, I don't use words. I allow the information to wash up into your body in quick waves.

You process: It is hard for whole-humans to survive childhood—after drought, war-poisons released into the air, strange virals. Many Gentry children die. Because cachemes are not whole-humans, Gentry can tinker with them in ways that give them a better shot at survival.

You feel the hot itch of desire. You wanted that rich girl to die. This is what your heart knows. You wanted her to die so that you could be called up into her life, which would become your own.

You feel wretched with guilt.

"That rich girl must have survived. Because I was re-lieved of my contract."

Yes.

"I was raised in a Ward of Cachemes. We were extras. We were made for the worst-case scenario."

Yes.

"I was created for the Kerr Family of Janix. They had a life together, one that I would never know."

You feel like you've been struck. Your eyes sting. I feel the blow. I absorb it.

"Was I born of a woman?" This seems important. You want something grounding, something you understand.

You were crafted, I tell you. *Then you were likely incu-bated inside of a woman. That woman may have been a cacheme repurposed for birthing.*

"Why can't cachemes know these things about them-selves? Why take away our pasts?"

I don't want to tell you anymore.

"Say it. Please."

Some cachemes hunted down their originals, ambushed and killed them so they could move into their lives. This is why they marked you with your scar. This way, cachemes cannot pass for their originals once their contracts are up.

You run your fingers down your scar. "But I'm not a kill-er." You think of all the cachemes in their glass boxes. Past versions turned violent. You want to wipe the scar away.

No. You change your mind.

"I want the Kerr Family of Janix to be forced to see my face. To see what they've done."

They may not have even survived. Before I was taken, there was already a surge of destruction. Battles between Gentry and revolutionaries. I was going to be taken into war when my boy grew old enough. This is how it was.

You feel your past, just out of reach. Your memories flutter like air-struck gills. I remember . . . I remember . . . I remember . . . You want the words to lead somewhere, anywhere . . . The emptiness is terrifying. You close your eyes. Faces seem to glide into your mind as if underwater—eyes-wide, breath-held, hands pulsing. But their features are blurred, indistinguishable. They wave to you. Are they all cachemes? Ones you grew up with?

"I see faceless faces."

You open your eyes. You feel a sharp pang. "How can I miss what I don't know?" A thought strikes you. "You knew we were in the Hellwash Mounds. Are you programmed with maps? Could you find Ward 147?"

Wards are private locations, not in my programming.

"But, if you could get at my memories, maybe we could see enough of the territory around Ward 147. Could we gather enough information to locate it?"

I am quiet. Then *I say, I could breach it. I could try. It could help. Hulls siphon neurons that fire off stray thoughts, daydreams, as well as basic functioning of the brain. Memory and imagination give us power.*

"Would it help you heal and grow strong?"

Yes, but recreating memories would take more effort. It will exact a harder toll on you.

"How?"

Hulls have a name for Gentry boys. We call them wicks. We use their lit minds as fuel. We have many sources of fuel, but their minds are the most powerful.

"The boys' minds burn like a wick in a candle, quickly?"

Yes.

"Is that why I feel weak? Is it because you've used my mind as fuel?"

Yes. But I needed it in order to protect you.

"I'm not just a wick to you. Am I?"

We are not that way. You rely on me and I rely on you.

You feel something like love. I feel something like love. Maybe neither of us are designed to understand love.

Only need. And we need each other.

You move your hands, watching the webbing roll over your fingers, over the bud bracelet. "How would you do it? How would you reach back into my memory?"

It is as if one finds only a feather from the wing of a bird. And from one feather, one can make a new bird. I can give you the new bird.

The image appears in your mind. Not a bird hatched from an egg. No. The feather is only that, soft and fine, a blue quill. But then as it embeds into a wing, the wing exists. And the wing stitches itself to a joint, unfurling bits of cartilage and bone, a frail casing of ribs to pro- tect—there it is: a small heart. The heart beats. Feather by feather, a body takes shape, a head appears. The beak grows at the same rate as the legs and claws. And, finally, there's the second wing. Both wings beat. The bird lifts. It isn't how birds are made. You know what I mean: From one small wisp, maybe I can construct a whole memory.

"I understand."

It will cause you pain.

You think about this. Ward 147 is only a vague notion. It may as well be just a cloud in a shape called home. You wish you could reconstruct it around yourself—founda- tion, beams, plaster. Cushions, bedsprings, and tubs. If you know home, you know who you once were within it. You could know yourself.

"How much pain?" You ask this, but the answer doesn't matter because you have already decided what you want.

There will be a lot of pain.

"I want to start. I'm ready."

I tighten my webbing. We cannot begin.

"What's wrong?"

A storm is coming.

"What kind of storm?"

I open an eye. A distant gust is coming in fast. It might be man-made. Far-off explosions can create roaring storms.

You see what I see.

Rusty wind, a blizzard of red snow. The wind shoves us against a rock. *We need better shelter.*

I push off of the rock and lean into the wind. My eye is quickly covered in rust. I blink but can't reopen it. I open another eye, but it too is quickly covered. Each eye offers barely a second of sight then it is gone.

I lumber forward, pushing against the wind, rust-blind. *Hold tight.*

The wind is powerful. I am weak from the journey. I lose my footing, shoving us backward. I pop open the claws embedded in my hooves. I dig in. We skid to a stop.

My joints are loose. My muscles wrung out. You are jostled in the webbing.

"How can I help? What can I do?"

I do not answer. There is nothing for you to do. The rust is getting deeper. I plunge through it.

And then a buzzing noise. My skin is pricked with pain. I am stung again and again. Around each small puncture, there is numbness, tingling. My brain offers a reading of their genus. These creatures are small but deadly. They feed on rust. They ride on storms. I have to get you to safety. Through to the other side of the storm. Where does it end?

Then you are stung too. The center of your palm, covered in webbing. The pain starts lightly but then the burning sets in.

I have been breached.

"Are there creatures burrowing in?"

Acidophiles. The rust isn't only rust. They live on rust and disguise themselves as rust.

"One stung me."

I cannot find shelter. I cannot find the edges of the storm. I turn back. Have I been turning a circle? The spots where I have been stung are now deadened. *Many have stung me. And the numbness has begun and the haze . . .*

"What haze?"

My mind is dimming . . . I can . . . I am . . . moving. I am . . .

"Are they going to kill us?"

I don't know, but there is numbness, haze . . .

You sense that you are losing me. You are terrified. Another sting hits you just above the knee. The burning spreads quickly up your thigh. I understand you. I do not understand the rust world.

I focus on your thoughts, hoping to find my thoughts. As if my thoughts can be hitched to yours and marched.

You are wondering if you were stung as a child. Bees. Whole hives of them, hybrids recreated for pollination dissemination.

They could swarm. What to do in a swarm? How to save yourself?

My voice is light and weak against your skin. *Bees, bees . . .*

You cannot rely on memory. You must rely on knowledge. My mind is slack. And pain fogs your thoughts, too.

Bees . . . If chased by bees, if surrounded by a swarm, what do you do?

And then it comes to you. Water.

A body of water.

The lake full of metal deposits and rocks. "Can you get us to the water?"

Water . . .

"Don't think. Just focus on water. Can you hear me?"

I sway.

"Just get to the water. Submerge yourself. We'll be safe."

I cinch the webbing and push into the rust-storm again.

I am still being stung. Hot and sharp. My body is slow. The rust is thick. I strain against the wind. The body of water. My internal maps are dim.

Another sting fires up your cheek, near your marking scar. The buzzing is louder, angrier. You are sweating, the webbing slick against your skin.

I am drawn to the water. I can see a bit of it ahead of me.

I push and push. My clawed hoof feels the ground soften. Then the coolness of water.

I throw myself forward. I move through the slushy rusty water. I am feeble. My mind must be nearly lost . . . my body is mostly numb. But I surge and, with one last sweeping movement, I arch.

We dip down and bob slowly back up.

We're floating.

Here, we bob and dip. The storm rages. I dive down. My claws stir the rusty silt. I lock my claws onto the lake bed. My body knows how to draw what it needs from water. I use a system like tiny gills. They open and flutter on certain stretches of my skin. I draw in the oxygen and feed it to you in the socket. I filter out the rust. We will stay below the surface. You say, "I want to name you. I want to thank you for everything, and I want to tell you things that are important to me. When I do, I want to say your name. And . . ." You are scared. "If we die, I want to have known your name."

I would tell you that I do not think we will die. But I cannot promise. I am sensing that this is a fevered place. I offer this instead. *If you go all the way back, before there were hulls, before there were mechas or mekanikaru or even giant robots, there were horses. There is the tale of a horse named Bucephalus. He was so great that when he died, a city was built and named for him.*

"We could name you for this great horse."

I am not worthy.

"We could name you like Bucephalus, but not exactly." You think about this. "How about Bukef."

I glow with warm light. It is not mechanized. It is organic. I love this name. To be in honor of but to be my own. *Bukef.*

"Thank you, Bukef. For everything."

The light grows warmer. You are welcome, I say and it means more than the simple politeness. It means you are welcome to stay within me forever.

You are still afraid of death, here in the Hellwash Mounds. I can sense that you want to know who you were before you die. I want to give you a gift because you have given me a gift. *Would you like me to try to return a memory to you now?*

"Yes, yes please."

This will be painful. Are you sure?

"I'm sure."

Try to be calm and still. I cup your head with my webbing. *I am going to engage different parts of your brain. I begin with your brainstem. It reminds your body to breathe, to digest, to pump your heart.*

Your organs tingle. Your heart valves flutter. Your lungs tighten as you exhale.

Do you have any part of your past? Has it come to you?

"Not really."

Your instincts are stored in the caudate nucleus.

Your brain is a lit globe. It shudders like heat lightning across a dark hot sky. Your hand feels like it is catching a ball, mid-air.

Your body's memories of how to walk and run and gesture are within the cerebellum.

Your legs start swinging wide, your hands spread against the webbing.

The occipital lobe.

Your mind sparks like a bright hot filament. A square of light. A striped square. Dust motes, fat and slow, spin idly.

"I think I'm remembering."

I see what you see. A window.

"Yes! Sun-struck. Almost blinding." The stripes come into focus. "A barred window."

The windows are barred so the cachemes couldn't jump.

"Is this my Ward of Cachemes?"

I do not know.

I take you through more lobes—frontal, prefrontal, parietal. I slip pulses into folds of gyri and the grooves of the cerebral cortex. You see: More light and dark, the spatial stretch of open air. The idea of a slope. Children's voices, loud and high-pitched.

But you want something full. Not just pieces.

With the swirling rust spinning in slow motion around us, I offer your brain a scent. You cannot name it, but you feel a new twinge. A swell of memory, just out of reach. "Do that again."

I do what I can. Scents pinprick your brain—sweet, sharp, acidic. They travel out, like winged insects among blossoms, but don't retrieve any memories.

There is no pain, but no memory either. Your mind feels hollow.

And then, set against darkness, a white puffy seed pauses, mid-air. It spins off.

"More like that," you say.

I keep the scents coming. Each one feels like a rising tide that ebbs.

Then, lime wash. Your right hand buzzes like it is scrubbing in circles—a thick brush, a wall with a bright pink splotch of mold. "We used lime wash to beat back the spores and wood-boring beetles." The scent hauls your past up like a drowning girl, your own mouth gasping at the surface. Your childhood face—maybe just ten years old, scrawny, big-eyed. No marking scar.

Your own sweet face scares you. You know that these memories will be tainted with sorrow.

I know that these things are coming and I want to spare you. *Do you want to keep going? It will get worse. Far worse.*

"I do."

I nestle down on the lake floor.

Honey-milk shampoo and lice powder . . . damp heads on pillows—cachemes in a row of cots. You see their shiny cheeks, faint smiles, eyebrows edged with tenderness . . . or is it fear? They're afraid for you. They don't want you to leave.

Burnish lotions rubbed into your skin to protect against the cancerous sun.

Wooliness, sweat . . . the proctors. They were cachemes too. Their scars were puckered and faded.

Mustiness—a game of hoops and stars being played in a basement, the rubber balls, the squeaking shoes, the high casement windows lighting the floor.

The powdery sugar and salt lacing the jellied eggs. The eggs fill your mouth, salty and sweet.

The memories hush in your mind. There's a lull. Your head fills with pain. When you close your eyes, you only see a bright light. Pain shoots down your limbs. It spikes in your joints.

You cry out. The cry vibrates in my body and imitates suffering.

The pain is like an animal that claws inside of you. It is a pain inside of me. You try to curl up. You feel the pain breaking up to the surface like a bright white.

We shouldn't have done this. My voice is just a whisper against your skin but it scrapes.

"Did you get a glimpse of the surroundings? Any clue to finding the ward?"

A little, yes. Through the window I could see a hill, woodlands.

"Keep going."

No. You must rest.

But now that the memories have begun, they keep going.

And there is pain. A foundation of it.

A scent forms a crack that bleeds light. It offers a sense of who you were.

You remember.

You are older, pulling a wheeler across the pocked yard of Ward 147. The wheeler is a heavy cart with a large cage. Wind kicks up seed-puffs. They stick to the high voltage-fence, the barred windows on the three-story building and the rust-mottled shed. You think: *Mine. This is mine.* The pain is ransacking your body. You refuse to give in.

The seed puffs dust a half-built go-go-roundy in the bald yard. The go-go-roundy is made of mute and frozen hybrid-horses. Their matted fur, exposed gears, and wiring have gone white. They will become a large toy that children ride.

We are not for you, the hybrids seem to whisper in the tinkling from the chime box. *We will never be for you.*

The proctors are building a go-go-roundy to see if they can sell it to Gentry. They always need more money. This is why you are setting out with the heavy wheeler—to find hybrids, the kinds that were once designed to hunt down rebels, immigrants, defectives. For the most part, the Gentry have won. And so, they let these hybrids power down and rot.

The pain comes at you in sharp blows: A gaunt hybrid in the go-go-roundy, propped against a shiny pole, seems to smile at you, sadly. Children in the yard are running around the go-go-roundy in the whirl of seed puffs. Their names come back to you: HarLE, Jinta, LO, and HA.

A hand rests on your shoulder. You know the hand.

Proctor Yelzbin. You know this name from the words in the cannister's lit air. Proctor Yelzbin wears her metal headdress that glints in sun. Her marking scar is thin and pale. The seed-puffs have laced her puffy hair as if with white flowers. Her eyes are dark. Her thin brows arched, expectant.

"Let's go!" she says.

Why you? Why not the others? You know that you are more trusted than they are.

You loved Proctor Yelzbin. You were afraid of her, too. "Wait," you tell me. "I need to take a break."

But I can't stop a memory as it rushes toward us. I try to, but there's only a gap, a hiccup. A jump forward . . . you and Proctor Yelzbin are beyond the fence, crossing the stubble field. I can see more landscape around the ward.

This is good.

You pull the wheeler and Proctor Yelzbin pushes it. The nubby wheels and our boots break stalks. The air fills with the chemically sweet rot of nerve gas, old layers and some that are still fresh. The Bloodbaths have bleached and suffocated everything. But this land is trying to beat its way back like someone paddling against a swift current. The woods at the top of the hill are greening.

We crest the hill. "Does this help?" you ask me. "A better view?"

Keep going.

You and Proctor Yelzbin push into the woods and come to a clearing filled with a herd of dead hybrids, some deer-like, some boar-like, but three are horse-like—exactly what the proctors need.

The hybrids seem to have found each other, as if awaiting a charge that never came. Their eyes have gone glassy. Decay has set in.

You two move among the herd. She touches a snout. You run your hands over antlers. Strange and beautiful. The pain is constant and it holds you, but you want to linger in this moment.

"You haven't chosen what to bring with you," Proctor Yelzbin says, her eyes are bright with tears.

"I don't want to be haunted."

The pain ratchets up quickly.

She opens her hand. There's the bracelet. "You should be haunted."

You turn it in your hands. Your contract will soon be up. You both know this. You will have to leave the Ward. You will be sent off. You will be marked with a marking scar. You will be repurposed. But this means something special. You twist the small knob, and the girl pops up, spinning.

After this memory, you collapse. You feel broken. You need time. I was close to locating the Ward. I have topography, flora and fauna. I am homing in. And I am getting stronger, fed by the synapses inherent in memory. The rapid firing.

The rust storm eases. On the surface, the wind has stopped ticking with rust and its settling to the bed more slowly. I unlock my claws. I kick off. We rise. I break the surface and open eyes in all directions.

The rust has been pushed out by heavy winds, leaving gritty traces behind. The sun is lost in the deep red clouds. The rust is deep. Banks of it line the ledges.

You are full of wonder. You don't understand this place. I don't understand this place. I don't know which direction to travel.

You are thinking the same thing. "Which way is home?"

We move back to our spot under the ledge.
We both sleep.

After many hours, I am lumbering around the edges of the clotted lake. I scan the horizon. Will we be safe here? I sense others, out there, somewhere. Are they drawing near? Will they be helpful or hostile?

You wake with a jolt. You tell me that you are ready to remember again. We do not need many memories. Hopefully the right ones will rise, the ones that will let us in.

I feed you scents. Dark memories spring open.

Back to a barred window. This time, it is night. Proctor Yelzbin pulls a pair of large scissors from her apron pocket. The metal headdress that cups her cheeks pokes out like blinders—a funnel directed to your ear. "You don't want to be sold off as a posey girl, Roon. Do you?"

"No," you say.

You know what posey girls do and the men who pay them to do it. You tighten your limbs, holding yourself close. You feel wound upon wound. Proctor Yelzbin wedges the scissors against the nape of your neck. Pulling your thick braid taut, she starts to cut. The scissors are so dull that they gnaw and gnaw. Your neck is taut, your head bobbing.

"You don't want to be an incubator, either," Proctor Yelzbin says. "You don't want to swell up with child after child, ones you never even get to hold."

"I don't," you say. "No."

The scissors cut through the final strands of hair. Your head jerks forward. She faces you. Her expression goes tender with loss.

Raw pain spasms in your chest.

Proctor Yelzbin says, "I cut all of the girls' braids. I keep them in a drawer to remember them. Cutting your hair will make them see you differently. Not as posey. Not as incubator. I hope that I have saved many from a dark fate."

You imagine the drawer. The braids. The girls . . .

"The hauler to take you to the space elevator will be here soon," Proctor Yelzbin says. "It's my job to prepare you to abandon me and to forget I ever existed."

She starts to cut the rest of your hair. The cold scissors knock against your skull. Wisps litter the floor. "But maybe you won't forget," she says softly. "Maybe you'll be different."

Light brightens the window. Proctor Yelzbin looks out. The hauler's engine hums louder as it draws near.

"Gather yourself," Proctor Yelzbin says. "It's time."

You draw in a wheeze then exhale raggedly. The pain is so intense that you think that you might lose consciousness. But you manage to say to me, "Look. Look out the window. Take it all in."

The pain presses in. It is loud and bright, a shock followed by another shock. But I do as you say. I pull my attention away from you and I look out the window.

Ward 147. It is far—past the Grip, past the cable, and the Wasted Plains. Southeast of here.

"You've got it?"

Yes.

I give you a small piece of the map. I pass it to you the same way my voice isn't heard but felt. It blooms in your mind.

The ward, the stubble fields to the west, leading to the wooded hill. The Wasted Plains, all around, and to the northeast the warehouse where you were taken in on the hauler, processed and shunted and marked, and bit farther north, the cable itself.

It still will not be easy, not for an escaped cacheme and hull, but I know where it is. We can stop now.

"Wait," you say, every inch of your body crying in pain. "The memory isn't over. There's more."

Later, Roon. Not now.

"Please! Now!"

My obedience kicks in. I offer exhaust and the smell of sweaty bodies.

You and Proctor Yelzbin are stepping off of the hauler. You walk in a line of cachemes—their faces not yet marked—and proctors, each marked with their scars. Guards stand nearby. Not far off, a warehouse. "This is where we said good-bye," you whisper to me.

Yes.

Proctor Yelzbin grabs your hand. She leans close and whispers, "Do not accept your fate. There will be a cage. It can come in many disguises. Do not accept the cage." Her eyes charged with fear. And then her gaze softens as if she's remembering something from long ago. "*Mo Roon,*" she says, and it sounds foreign, full of longing.

Your body is still seized with pain. The memory is gone. You are crying and writhing in the webbing. "*Mo Roon, Mo Roon . . .* what does it mean?"

I am silent.

Someone is coming. Maybe more than one.

"What is it?" I have tensed and you sense it.

We are not alone. There are others.

Through one of my eyes, you look out into the ruddy wind. At first the landscape seems empty. A flat stretch with rust-blurred ridges. Others? Out here? It doesn't seem possible. "Nothing can be alive out here."

Listen.

You hear growling engines and move to another eye. Three swirls of dust on the horizon. Three specks emerge, peeling away from the red terrain. They are old corroded tanks coated in rust. Remnants from a very old war. Guns strapped to them. Old hybrid skins stretching taut over holes and aged joints. The fur of the stitched-together hides is gritty with rust.

"Have they noticed us?"

Yes.

"Can we outrun them?"

No.

"What do they want?"

You.

You pull yourself away from my eyes. "Why do they want me?"

They assume a rich Gentry boy is within.

"I'm not rich. I'm not a boy. I'm not Gentry."

They don't know that.

Your heartbeat is quick. I feel your pulse in your fists.

I won't hand you over. We are. Not you, not me. We are.

The engines are so close the roaring vibrates the webbing. It shivers over your skin. The air is agitated.

You put your face close to one of the eyes and see a tank's grill and hand-rigged guns. Its hovercraft air-blasts are weak and uneven so it bottoms out, nicking and banging against the ground.

One tank is in front. The other two, on either side, stay twenty feet back, their engines idling.

A hatch opens, metal grinding on metal.

An oversized, partially cleaved bald head emerges. He's a twinner—his face slightly doubled. Mouth-wide, too many teeth, a broad nose with a large cleft, a set of eyes that begin and start to end but then begin again—four total. His head is too big and stuffed into a thick neck. There were many twinners created and released. They were Gentry test-tube attempts at trait-upgrades that didn't work. Most embryos were erased but some were raised for further testing. No need to mark them with a scar. They are obviously not originals. His face is boiled. His machine gun and bullet sashes seem old-world.

Like the tank itself, his skin is coated in rust and so he bleeds into the landscape.

He climbs on top of the tank. He is quick despite his bulk. Dead bugs are stuck to the tank's coating of rust. Their bodies are gone, only wings remain.

The twinner sits on the tank, legs dangling. He stares at me. "Damn, I only *heard* of things like you. Rumors." He squints. "You got a little dinged up didn't you, pretty boy?"

I am not his boy. I am not a boy. Between you and me, I did not have to be male or female. I could simply be. And now I am *boy*. I am reduced, as if I am a child, as if he owns me in some way and can call me what he wants. I hold *boy*. I hold it and I am silent, unmoving.

"You're going to die out here, you know that?" He brushes off rust from his hands. They are blackened with oddly shaped dark cancers. One finger's been amputated completely. "You've got to come to terms with death in the Hellwash Mounds." He rubs one hand over his bald head and smiles. He steps down onto a flat part of the tank and swings a large tank-mounted gun around. You move to another eye for a view.

He points the gun at me. "I don't think you're going to do us much good," he says. "Unless you got a prize inside."

I remain completely still. The other two tanks cut their engines. Those within know they're going to stay a while. "What should we do?" you whisper. Your breaths are quick and light.

I am silent. It is my answer.

The twinner unlocks a metal hook and the muzzle slides closer to my hide. He jerks it to a stop. He seems to make sure it is loaded. He hits a button and a thin red beam connects the muzzle to me.

"Why don't you be nice and open up so we can see what you got?"

I contract.

"Come on now." The twinner maneuvers the gun again and the muzzle glides on its long arm, poking into my flesh. "Knock, knock," he says. "Open wide."

I do not respond.

"Open up!"

The hatch on one of the other tanks clanks open. He is not a twinner and not whole human. He is a jiq. I have seen them as babies, hanging in nets at market stalls when I was my boy's hull. Their skin was not supple enough to be pinched by the netting. They rasped when they cried out. Their respiration mechanisms were always purring and ticking. This jiq is a basic model. Part-DNA but mostly man-made and rough-hewn. His ears lack intricate whorls. His eyes stutter. They blink too hard. His nose and mouth are covered in a respirator, much like the tank's grill. It digs into the skin under his eyes and puckers his neck.

He pushes his way up from the hatch. His chest—broad and ripped—is covered in a see-through box strapped to his shoulders. Is the box made of bullet-proof glass? It offers a view of his internals. He has no skin beneath the box—only ribs protecting two black pumps working like lungs. Pleated, the pumps constrict and relax, constrict and relax. Thin tubes connect the box to his respirator. He is fat-chested and almost too big for his lung-box. It is as if he's outgrown it. The meatiness of his sides presses against the glass, bulging around its edges.

He has a head of bristly hair.

The twinner spins around and shouts, "Catwald, I told you to stay in the tank!"

Catwald looks at me. "I had to see it! I never seen a live one before this, you know. Only that dead one. And it was long dead. It took on a stench."

"Cattie, I've got it covered. I don't need you out here."

"Is he almost dead? He seems almost dead. I don't think he's got anything inside him or he wouldn't look like that."

"I have this under control, Cattie. Get back in the tank."

"He's like a skull, for sure. Almost dead," Cattie says. "Don't shoot him though. You might pop what's inside. But I doubt he's got anything in there. Like I said, Merce. He's like the other one we found. He'll start to stink soon. You should just open him up yourself. But don't shoot him."

"Are you telling me to gut him?" Merce shouts. "*You* gut him if you want to gut something."

The third tank opens and a bony woman emerges. Her head is also shaved. She wears goggles tinged blue. A tumor has risen in the center of her chest. She has no lung-box. Only a respirator. It is caked with so much rust that it can't let in much air. She is neither a twinner nor a jiq. I do not know what she is. "I'll gut him," she says.

"I told you all to stay in your tanks!" Merce says.

"I'm being courteous," the woman says. Her voice holds no emotion. "No one wants to gut the thing, and I will."

"You should let her," Cattie says. "You should."

"Shut the hell up!" Merce presses his hands to his ears, straining the respirator straps in a way that warps his face. "Shut up!" He stands there like a rusty statue for a moment.

Then he screams, long and loud.

He takes a deep breath and says to the woman, "Gut him."

You turn away from the eye and whisper, "What are we going to do?"

I am not almost dead. Be still. Be calm. I will not let them take you.

Compression overhead, the woman's boots. I open an eye near what would be my interlocking vertebrae. You can see the bony woman's face—her sunken cheeks and jaw cut into by her respirator. Her cheeks rise a little like she's smiling, but her mouth is blocked by the respirator's rust-gummed grill.

Then you see the knife raised over her shaved head. The wipers on her goggles blink ferociously.

I see it too.

My webbing courses with electrical pulses. And your skin flashes with heat. You feel like you are being scalded. "What's happening?"

This is temporary.

The woman drives the knife down but then stops. My body crackles and there's a deafening jolt of electricity.

The woman's hand is still gripping the knife, but her face has gone rigid. Her body shudders violently. Her goggles jerk away from her eyes, which have rolled back in her head. Her lids flutter. Her eyes shine moon-like.

Cattie cries out.

The woman goes limp and falls.

Your skin starts to cool. This exchange has taken great energy. My inner light goes out. All of my eyes close. Your hearing is muffled. You don't know if Cattie and Merce are trying to revive the woman or if she's already on her own two feet, coming to.

After a few minutes, the tank engines rev and move on, past us.

I go slack. My body twitches like someone deep in dreams. My neurological system is on minimal drive. I must recover.

You start shaking. Your arms thrash. You replay what happened in your mind. Your mind homes in on the insect wings stuck to the rusty metal. Insects are an indicator of life.

"Should we follow the tanks' tracks back the way they came?"

Yes. I know the way to go. But not yet. Not . . . I am reserving energy. I am powering down to a lower level.

You want to help me. I am inert. I am trying to barely exist and yet still hold you. And you know what helps: To retrieve a memory to feed me.

But you doubt you can do this on your own.

You are searching for a small beautiful memory. Something good.

You don't have to . . . you . . .

One surfaces. At first just slick grass. Sun wavering . . . You and Proctor Yelzbin have filled the wheeler's cage to the brim with hybrids for the go-go-roundy. As you are walking across a stalk field, you hear a chattering chorus far off.

You stare at each other, afraid. Her pupils dilate to the very edges of her irises.

The noise grows louder and then chaff eaters appear in a gusty cloud, bringing with them the scent of the far-off ocean. Their tiny wings chitter. They billow and kick up a dusty breeze and fly toward you.

And you hand yourselves over. No reason to fight. The chaff-eaters cover every bit of our exposed skin. Their tiny mandibles are nibbling the stiffened coat of burnish lotion that helps protect cachemes from sun. They seem to be polishing you. Your bodies are alive with the mad flutter of wings.

You are lost in a gnawing cloud that, when it lifts, leaves you new and clean.

The memory is alive on your skin. I sense it. My webbing tingles with recognition.

My voice is a light sweep over your skin. *I felt your memory. I felt it within.* The webbing trembles. I know much about you. But I have not told you about me. I am filled with a desire to confess. *I killed a boy. He was a wick within a hull. I killed the hull too.*

You don't try to imagine it. You don't allow it in. You simply say, "You're good, deep down." You know that I would never hurt you just as I know you would never hurt me.

We know each other, I say. *We are bound.*

You are strong and powerful. I recover quickly and we begin our journey. We know where Ward 147 is. We move toward it. It will be a long journey. The air is still thick. Pockets of red chalk billow up. But we come to a stretch where the air is calm and clear.

You want to feel the sun and air on your skin. "Can I get out?"

It will never be entirely safe, but now is a good moment. I open my vertebrae so you can climb out.

We walk side by side. You are bone-tired but it feels good to squint into the sun. You keep one hand flat on my side. Tethered. "It's strange to be solitary again."

Yes. I do not prefer it. I am not as much use. But I know that this is what you need.

"Why did Proctor Yelzbin say *Mo Roon*? Why am I called Roon?"

I know the language of every wick that might climb inside of me. Roon *has many meanings in languages new and old.*

"Too many to guess?"

The word has different roots but it can mean letter, literature, secret. *Another root means* to roar, murmur, mumble, whisper. *It can mean* a poem, a song, an incantation, a spell. *But Proctor Yelzbin uses two words. The first is* mo. *In a language used long ago by people far, far from here,* mo *meant* my *and the pronunciation of a word spelled* r-u-n, *with an accent over the* u, *was pronounced* roon. *The way she said it, it may come from this language, the one that used it as an endearment. My mystery.*

"I'm a mystery now, to myself. Was I a mystery back then too?"

I don't know.

The flat land gives way to hills. Grasses, moss, and lichen have muscled up from the dirt.

After a while, you get tired. I lower myself, and you climb up on my back. The vertebrae have receded. I am so broad that it is easier to ride on my back cross-legged. Your hair has grown out a little. It is ruffled by the wind. Your shirt too— it ripples against your skin. The sun, unchecked by rust, is hot.

We make our way along the ridge of a hill toward the peak in hopes of a view. Hundreds of feet below, a spread of wild terrain. The return of knuckled roots. Vines stretch out through brush and bushes. Saplings are wedged in among cobbled forests, blackened by the nerve gas of old wars. Laid to waste by viruses, war, polluted air, the brutal sun. New Bloodbaths have begun. They have not touched down here. Not yet.

In the distance a cloud of green bugs rises. They are the ones you saw on the tanks' grills. A light cloudy mass of them undulates and drifts across the new fields. They thread in and out of skinny trees. They ride along the dry riverbed, never touching down.

Farther out, they float toward a bustling city.

The Grip. The suburbs are beyond it. Shining bubbles that cap each small town.

"Is one of them Janix where the Kerrs are from?"

Yes.

"Did you live in one of the bubbles?"

Yes, with my wick and his family. But I was defective. I was a killer. I was taken away.

"Tell me about the boy."

My skin tightens and goes cold.

"I'm sorry. I don't mean to upset you."

I open an eye upon my back and look up at her.

Are you sure you want to hear?

"Yes. I'm sure."

My wick was strong. He was decisive. He had enemies. Other boys he hated. Other boys who hated him.

"Did you love him?"

I did not know love. I knew obedience. And loyalty. I was supposed to serve him. To keep him safe.

"Did you?"

I did but it went too far.

"What happened? Can you tell me?"

On High Field beyond the bubble. It was dark. Two boys in hulls. Other boys circled, ripped off puffed ties and shoved them in pockets. They took bets. Girls in veils stood at the edges.

"A fight?"

A duel. A small boy in the field held a white towel in the air. He dropped it and ran. He wore short pants and one sock drooped low.

You are imagining the story as I tell it. Your mind is crisp and clear. You see the boy's skinny calf, the white towel flashing in the dark.

My wick told me to charge. We were one. My wick hated the other wick. That boy was drunk and so his hull was in a daze. Its knee locked. It fell. We kept coming. I wanted to stop. My wick wanted to form a claw. We did.

My wick wanted to rip the other hull open, slice the web within. We did.

My wick wanted a horn to hook the throat of the hull and the boy, to split them both. We did.

"You had no choice," I say.

I have a will of my own. It grew small.

"You can't blame yourself."

I should have stopped him.

"What happened then?"

The other wick had a brother. He cried for help. And the little boy picked up his white towel. He held it tight.

My wick told me to turn away, to shut all eyes. But I kept one open.

The other wick was still within his hull, strung up by the webbing. His brother leaned into the dying hull and shouted at the hull to release his brother's body.

The hull went limp. Its back opened. The brother gripped the wick's legs and pulled him out from the hull like a colt, born breech and dead.

"You had no choice," you tell me again.

They say a hull can't stop a wick. But I know I can. I am strong. If I don't believe this then I am not my own. And I can't ever be my own. We share this.

"What do you mean? What do we share?"

We belonged to others. But we made a choice.

It is true. You recall being in the glass box. You made a choice to get out. The others did not.

We walk back down from the peak. The land rolls out beneath us. A sloping, barren hill gives way to a pale, green field. Grasses bow in the wind, folding into yellows. A bright haze.

"I need to run. To feel my body is my own."

I understand.

A fissure splits within your chest, bursting wide. You climb off my back and start to run downhill with great momentum, toward the greenery. Your legs can barely keep up. Your arms pump and then spread for balance.

The sky is clear. The sun a brilliant flare. And you are fast.

I know that this is what's happening within you: Blood rushes to your head, thunders in your chest.

I follow. I must. I run as fast as I can and it feels good. I smell what you are smelling. The kicked-up earth, the old rust lightly chuffing from your shirt and hair, the far-off scent of the greenery exhaling its pollen. I also smell the foulness of my own body airing.

At the bottom of the hill, you come to the edge of the green field and stop. You turn and see me.

I am barreling down the hill after you. On all fours, I feel muscular, my skin tensile and shining. My coloring has shifted to blend with the dirt. But because you are there, gazing at me, I grow ebony horns as ornate as fluted shells but enormous. My head is majestic, large and sleek. I have opened a curved row of eyes. I want to see everything.

My hoofs pound the dirt. Rough clouds and clods rise up. But these hoofs have claws, thick and sharp. I become more mechanical with some internal engine, precision, speed. But also, I am more animal. I careen toward you then pivot and leap. I circle back and slow to a stop.

I bow my head.

You reach up and touch a black horn.

We both look out across the green field. It goes on and on, grasses rippling.

"It's like an ocean," you say.

Out across the green field, the wind blows and the pollen drifts. "Do you know what I'm afraid of?"

Tell me.

"I'm afraid that they will take this away from me, too, one day. This memory. You and me. Us. Here."

I will hold this memory for you. You and me. Us.

You feel lit up. A brightness glows in your chest and warms your cheeks. "When you started to run, I didn't know it. But the air seemed to tremble. I thought that I was the cause of the trembling, as if my banging heart could stir the wind. But it was you." You look at me, eyes wide. "Can you run like you just did with me inside of you?"

With you, I can run faster.

"That's not possible."

We should try.

You want to run straight into the field, across the velvety green, kicking up pollen in billowy gusts. "Let's cut across it."

Yes.

You climb back inside of me. The webbing weaves around your legs and arms, around each finger. I open eyes all around you so you have a view of the land in every direction.

I tilt forward, and you lean with me. And I tear into the field.

As I gather momentum, you look straight ahead and out of the eyes on either side. The landscape shifts as we settle into a steady stride. You move your legs like you are running. You pump your arms. For every one of your strides, I take at least four. You push harder, and soon, for each of your strides, I take eight or more. You feel almost weightless, smooth and fleet. We're in sync, a rhythm of infinite gears and pounding hearts and synapses. We grow stronger and stronger.

The scenery clips by. We are not galloping as much as gliding. We flush birds up into the sky. You remember the way I explained how I would return your memories to you—from one wing, we would create a whole bird. You imagine the full bird, its puffed chest, its two wings flapping. You feel like we could fly.

On the other side, we arrive in a stubble field. It holds less green. More rattling stalks. This is when I sense my ancestor from the Old World. I know his body is near before I see it. I slow and you ask, "What's wrong?"

Nothing is wrong. But we must stop.

I move forward slowly. The land slants downhill. Then I see him. You do too.

He lies on his back in the stubble field. His mechanical body was big enough to hold a crew of three. But his bronze skull is cracked. Weedy green stalks shoot up through his bare ribs.

A breeze dusts up fine metal flakes from his rust. Motes spin in harsh sun. He is long dead, one of the fallen.

"What is this?"

A soldier.

You are shaken because I am shaken.

I walk closer.

Bullet holes pock what is left of his shield-skin. He has been hollowed by weather. Rotted clean. There are no wires, no more weaponry. His bullet sashes have been plucked. He has been gutted by pickers and hybrid beasts. They know how to scrape every bit of use from a derelict body.

His heavy boots once tread the land like an immortal. Now his boots are slack, cocked wide.

You want to get out. I open. You climb up from my webbing and walk around the fallen giant. He is an old, abandoned model of hull, an early version.

"He was so strong." You mean, *Is it hard to see him like this? Are you afraid of this kind of death?*

I tell you what I know of my ancestral line. *They were strong and brave. They were vulnerable. I was designed differently. Made to mimic more of the natural world. I am a model made in their image, but other images too.*

His eyes are gone. The sockets dark. It is as if the holes cannot see but know how to gaze. I open an eye on my back to look up to see his view—days shifting to nights. Of sun then stars. The slow turn of the planet, holding him in place.

I am machine. I am mammalian and reptilian with touches of humanness, born from a wet mold and hand-wired, hand-stitched to endure. But I know my heritage. I come from fallen giants. The old soldier—warrior of the Old World—was honorable.

I turn to you. I want to capture you in the gaze of one of my multifaceted eyes the way I did that first time we met. I knew then that I needed you and you needed me.

You put your hand on my side.

I will, one day, be abandoned like a fallen giant in a field. I will wither and fade. My network will be rooted to dirt, weed by weed—a new kind of wiring.

We will always wonder if there is more to us, if we were granted a self or if we are like this one—made to be of use and left to rot. Maybe we cannot know what is what.

This is how you respond to me. Some weeds are dotted white. You pick these flowers. A ragged bouquet. You put the white flowers on what remains of the soldier's metal chest plate. The spot where his heart once might have beaten.

I tell you the one truth I am certain of. *Without you, there is no me.*

"Together, we're something that doesn't exist anywhere else. We're something no man could ever imagine or manufacture. We are."

We are.

We have to travel around the Grip. It is blocked by an enormous wall of tall spikes that buzz with electricity. We pass an entry point. Booth that has been abandoned. We do not want entry. We keep our distance with a view of the Grip's skyline through a haze of smoke. There has been a lot of damage since we were shipped off. It has grown brittle. The cable itself is lost. Severed.

The outskirts are desolate. And I am thankful. Far off, a bomb detonates. A pillar of smoke shoots up and feathers across the sky. It erases what remains of buildings, two spires, a metallic tube-bridge.

I show you the bubble neighborhood that was Janix. It has been torched. What remains is skeletal scaffolding.

Two more bubble membranes covering adjacent neighborhoods have turned to char. One is currently burning. Pieces peel loose, sail and kick in the wind. The neighborhoods are laid bare, dotted with fires. The air shivers with ash and embers.

A herd of loose, wild hulls stampedes toward us. They are too frantic to notice us. Slick bloodied horns and hoofs, hulking weight, trembling muscles. Their bodies covered in eyes.

One of the hulls lets out a violent cry.

Another hull returns the call.

The rest join in.

Their roars fill the air.

"What are they saying? What do they mean?"

Let us alone. Let us go. This is what they want.

I cannot stop myself. I cry out too. It builds in my chest and feels ripped from my throat.

One of the last hulls in the herd slows. We gaze at each other through smoke. We see ourselves in each other's eyes. And we mourn. We are no longer who we were. We cannot become new.

I carry you away from the Grip, the fallen cable, the ruins. Into the Wasted Plains. We must pass through them to get to the Ward. Smoke still floods the dark sky over the Grip. The fires are behind us. You fall asleep. Your neurons burst, in dreams, with fear and loss. I siphon this neural energy and use it for fuel. We will need this. I fear for what is ahead. We move onward through the night.

In the morning, you haven't woken. The ash is gone. The air smells of the blistering agents of nerve gas.

The Wasted Plains are made of dirt like scaly imbricate skin. Each step creates fissures. The fissures open the worlds of creatures that live below. Mammalian heartbeats. Insects with twitching antennae. Underground earth eels chewing tunnels through parched dirt. I sense them all—skittering, writhing, eating darkness.

Sometimes I spot a few vacant hulls. They are aimless. An eye here or there, dazed. They are hungry. Startled, they run. Others carry wicks. Their eyes flash. They are running away.

As we move through the plains, things emerge.

Clusters of scrub bulbs.

Circuits of vines.

A stretch of dry grass bent to wind.

The sun rises higher.

We crest a hill.

On the other side, a herd of hulls in an abandoned uranium tank field. They rest in the shade of old holding tanks and the massive wells with caged caps. The tanks are weed-rimmed. The smell is tannic and sulfurous.

There are cavities where cylindrical tanks once were. Muddy toxic impressions.

Sensing me, the hulls turn their large heads. Their eyes appear.

These are not like those in the wild herd that cried out. These have been let loose for some time. The hulls are battle-worn. Some still blood-caked. Some wounded, burned. Jagged from bullet holes. Dark cavities gape open. They look at me like they're hungry. Hulls, in their natural state, don't want to be vacant. They want a wick. They know I have a wick within me. I know they are empty. They hunger for something to hold.

I cinch my webbing. Wake, wake.

"What is it?" I open a few eyes near you. "What is it?" You look out.

Blanklookers. I open eyes on the other side of my body. You see the glint of metallic skin, barbed horns, muscular haunches.

They are imbalanced, lost. They want a wick, like you.

"Do you have a plan?"

There are too many of them.

"But you've got me. We're stronger than blanklookers."

They're unwell. They have been through too much.

"They're worn down. They've had no fuel for a long time. They're lost and hungry. Disoriented probably."

A hull roars and pounds a hoof against the ground.

I bow my head.

"Are you giving in?"

The hulls start to circle. *I must draw them close.*

One hull knocks into me. Another shoves me with a horn.

"Will they kill you to get at me?" You take a handful of the webbing and pull yourself forward.

I know only that the hulls won't kill you. They will want you for fuel.

One shoves me so violently that I lose my balance. I grunt and right myself.

You imagine the herd tearing into me. Our helplessness. "If you let me out, I can cause a distraction. I can get help."

No. I will not let you go.

"We're going to lose each other either way. They'll kill you."

Then I will die fighting to save you.

I look inward and see your face. It is like you were invented out of thin air—your eyes, your face, your delicate ears. My mind feels like it is dilating, opening up to draw in more of you.

"There has to be something we can do."

You should know how to get home. Without me. In case . . .

You feel a sensation shoot across your skin and then the ward itself appears in your mind. It is on a map.

I draw in a deep breath and rear back onto my hind legs. I stand like the old soldiers before me stood, proud and strong. On two legs, I stretch myself as tall as I can. I puff my chest. Spikes rise across my skin. I grow a set of sharp and glorious horns. I roar as if it is my last.

And then I fight. For you. For us.

I am stronger. But they are many. They circle and lunge. They try to spear and gut me. I rip a few.

And I am wounded, too. The wounds perforate my hide. I am bloodied.

I feel smaller and smaller. They overpower me. They have gotten hold of the seam on my back and are trying to dig their way in. To you. I buck and kick.

Stay small. Huddle.

You are too scared to speak.

I fight as hard as I can, but they pin me to the bloody oily earth. I stare straight up.

The sun, a swollen contusion, stares down at us—a bright burning gaze. I want to gouge out the sun's eye so its crying light.

I sense the hulls pulsing with fear and anger, a desire for mercy. Every wound feels like a memory. There are no new bruises—only old bruises, relived.

We are of dirt and blood and oil. My thoughts feel muddy. I am full of dust and air. My body is chalky. But for this moment, I am not thinking of you, Roon. I am thinking of the hulls. I am thinking of how we were made and why. And how we came to be here.

Look at us, I think. *We are all of the same maker. A maker who did not love us enough. A maker who cheated us of our own will, of love. We should be free.*

The hulls pause. They eye me.

Dizzy and sick, I keep going. *We carry our maker's violence. He is inside of our chests. This beating pulse is part his. This thought in my head is part his. This tightness in my chest is part his. Our blood, brains, muscles, these are all part his.*

They release me and back away. They have never heard a hull speak this way. I would not know how except that I have known you. I have known love. I stagger to get my claws under me. A few hulls growl and lumber. I lift my face to the sun. I open my mouth to drink it up. The sun is too bright. My eyes feel bitten and sore.

The hulls stare at me. They make noises that come up from their throats. They tense and shift closer. They don't want you. They want more from me.

I tell them what I want to happen to me, what I want to happen to all of us. *Take this maker out of us! Rip him from our bodies! Let us be who we are. Let us be!*

My voice is like a needle threading the herd together, stitching them tight. This feels good. They buck. They push against each other—in anger? They seem constricted. Their voices trapped.

Set us free, I say. *Set us free of the makers who claim us.*

The hulls bellow. They pitch their bodies into each other. They each seem like a collection of parts. Some wail. My body feels bright. Like I did drink the sun. I imagine the glow. I wonder if I am shining.

A hull's head weaves into view. It might take me apart, piece by piece. But then, like the others, it lists away. My ears ring, and then the ringing sounds far off.

I hear a whine overhead.

The air fills with a damp fog. Nerve gas. The Bloodbaths have rippled out from the city. We are being doused by a cargo plane. It buzzes past and is circling back. The hulls are dazed by it. I hear your voice. "Run," you say. "Now. Save us. Run."

I run.

The air is hot. I cut through it, but the heat seems to bind everything together. Sky to leaf to horn and back again.

You see the cargo plane, its release of fog. You ask me what it is.

Nerve gas designed to kill hulls.
"Do you feel any effects?"
No.
"Who wants to kill hulls?"
Revolutionaries do. The Gentry use us for war.
"But you don't want to be used by Gentry for war."
Revolutionaries don't know what we want or who we are. They see us as the weapons we were made to be.
"Will you be okay?"
I will take you. I am fine.

The nerve gas is still diluted. The wind helps. But clouds ahead are forming a seal, capping the gas. When it rises, it will be pushed back down again.

I focus on you. Your heart propels us. I am programmed for loyalty. But loyalty may be a form of love. I don't know if one emotion can combine with others and grow like fresh ganglia, like spindle neurons. I know that I understand love. I feel love for you.

The sun brightens the smoke and gases. I brace for signs of exposure. I measure my vitals. All are stable.

We charge uphill. Behind us, the uranium tanks and cage-capped wells are in view. Many hulls are dead. Some run wildly. They are nearly lost in dust and gas. Some stampede. They run and veer in unison like flocks of birds.

One group runs through toxic mud. They stagger and fall.

A lone hull climbs onto the edge of a massive well. It bucks as steam rises from its skin. It pitches backward. The well's covering holds its weight for a moment and then snaps loose. The hull disappears.

The hulls' bodies shake rigidly. They knock against each other and the dirt.

I keep checking for a breach of my nervous system. I keep running. We head toward the woods. We are getting closer to the Ward.

You gaze at the passing trees. You see a patch of white flowers, wet and clotted. You remember a cluster just like these, rooted in mud. "I've been here." You move frantically from one eye to another.

"Proctor Yelzbin took me to these woods. She trusted me. This is where we hunted hybrids."

Up ahead, there's a clearing. Spores ride lightly through the air.

"This is where we found the herd of hybrids that had powered down. I am sure of it."

You look out in the direction I know will take us to the Ward. "The path has been covered in vines but it's still there."

A sharp metallic burn is breaching my skin. It is sudden. It takes root in the filigree of my sinuses. I want to barter with nerve gas, with air and sunlight. I want the wind to kick in. I want to rewind time, the way I have observed you as you skitter backward in a memory then repeats an image over and over until it finally seems smooth.

I falter.

I remember you in the space elevator, the blue glow of the emergency light, having come to save me.

"Bukef?"

I am aware of the liminal space between us. We aren't one. We never were. I sense you suddenly not as corporeal but made of opalescent air.

"Is it hitting you?"

I hear your voice. Strange music too. I smell something fragile. I sense a taste. Something dirty and metallic.

I am not made of body. I sense myself, and I am not myself. I can't take a step but I am moving, sliding.

You need to get out.

"No, I will stay inside of you. You'll need me to heal."

I do not want to die with you locked inside of me—like the dead boy on High Field. The one I killed. The one who had to be pulled from his hull.

I concentrate on my vertebrae. It takes all of my will to open.

But you will not leave. You lock your arms and brace your legs. "You need me. I will feed you memories. I will create fuel for you!"

I constrict my webbing and try to force you out.

"No!" You shout and cling. "If we follow the path, we'll come to a stalk field. We can run across. We can run like you and I did in the green pollen fields. Remember? We can be there tonight."

I want to obey you. I want to let you stay. But I cannot let you. Last time, I obeyed the wick. I didn't assert my will. A boy and a hull died. I must do what is right for you even if you do not want it.

I push harder.

You grip the webbing.

I continue the pressure. And finally, I sense you tumble forward to the ground. I am vacant.

You are shouting, "We're so close! We can make it together. I will walk alongside you. Proctor Yelzbin will help you when we arrive."

You are a flame. A bright luminescent flame. Who speaks.

"I'll go with you. You'll need me to heal!" Your face is wet. It shines.

I understand something that I have known for some time but did not want to be true.

I will not be able to be a hull among cachemes. Cachemes are overseen by Gentry. I am a defective. I will not be able to be hidden away.

They might be able to take you back. This is what I believe: Proctor Yelzbin wanted you to come back to her. I don't know why. But she did. And she will be happy to see you.

You will have to choose. And I do not want you to have to make a choice. You might choose me. But you might regret it. You could live your life missing your own people, your home.

"Can you hear me?"

I can hear you. I can see you. I am not my body, but I tell my body to turn around and my body turns.

What I mean is, *I love you.*

What I mean is, *I will die for you.*

You run after me, reaching up. You grab my knotty vertebrae. Your feet swing and knock against my hide. "You need me! Let me back in!"

I retract the knotty bones into my skin and let you fall to the ground.

"Please!"

I want you to give up. But you run after me, pounding on my side. "Let me in!" You are as wild as the dying hulls.

I don't stop. I run with a limp and stagger.

You keep up with me. You claw me. "Look at me!" It is more roar than human. "Stop! Wait!"

I don't stop.

You are breathless. You fall to your knees. "Bukef!"

I move through the woods with as much speed as I can. Each tree strikes me as pure love that is root-wired to the earth. Love that cannot be moved or given. Love that is locked in place.

What happens to love that cannot escape? The wind-kicked trees throw their limbs around. They are suffering. They are crying for help.

My body is trapped in a halo of pain. A coffin made of the sun. Light ripples and shakes, convulsively. I see the edges of light being gnawed by darkness. The sun is bitten and bitten. Finally, just a small wafer of light still exists.

I open my mouth to taste it.

I think, *Good-bye. Good-bye.* I know you are too far away to know what I've said.

I feel like a child who can barely speak. I think, *Bye-bye.*

I push myself to the edge of the trees and, once there, amid all of the tethered, frantic love, I give in. I have to shut down. The leaves are each held to the other by heat. My vision, in all directions, blinks and flutters shut.

Blinks and flutters shut.

The trees can't contain their love. Each one bursts. And bursts.

The sun is a bright oval door that swings shut.

*

You do not let me go. You follow the trail of oily blood. You move away from the trail, the ward, your home. You keep going farther and farther into the woods.

You imagine the herd of hulls, all dead. The nerve gas sweeping across the plains, rolling over their bodies. You wonder: Can hulls heal themselves once the nerve gas gets in? Some must be able to. They must. Still you imagine their eyes glazed and still. An unseeing eye is a terrifying eye. It sees through you.

The trees seem contorted. Their leaves thick and choked. Their limbs arched and pained. The breeze rustles through them in a muffled and chalky way. You cross your arms, pinching your own skin. You are angry that I kept going. That I left you.

You hear growling engines overhead. Through the limbs, you can make out cargo planes roaring in. How many? You cannot tell.

You move faster now, almost throwing yourself forward. Gnats whir in the air. Insects shoot up from a cracked stump. The nerve gas has disturbed everything.

You worry that I have wandered off to die. You start to run. A full sprint.

Then you stop, breathless. A few gnats flit into your gasping mouth.

I am there, before you and not. You run to me, collapsing to your knees.

My body already looks much smaller. My skin is dry

and dusty with what looks like a layer of charcoal.

It is getting closer to sunset. The light takes on gold. Your hands are trembling. You touch my skin. It has become turgid. You refuse to believe that I am dead.

And I am not.

"You did this once before. You threw that electrical force field around your body to protect us out in the Hellwash Mounds. You were damaged then too." You run your hand along my back, searching for the vertebrae. "You just need to open so I can get in."

Your hands pat my skin frantically. The char-like film covers your palms. You hate the feel of it. "There it is. An eye." You have found one dim eye on my shoulder. "You can see me! You are going to be okay." Your voice trembles.

I can see. But my view is dull and gray.

And then my frame contracts. The charcoal dust pops loose as I get smaller, more leathery.

"Let me in. Do you hear me? I can help you."

I cannot be helped now. I am powering down. It is the final option of repair. You can see it that, beneath my skin, ridges have formed. Between the ridges, I am sunken, fibrous and hollow.

Your touch becomes skittish and light.

More contractions. They startle you. I am becoming essential, smaller and tighter.

"I'll take you with me to the Ward. We can still go, together."

I cannot move. I am too large to carry. You know this.

But you are not rational. You are still crying. You wipe your face of tears, a rough gesture. You stand and turn a small circle. Tree-limb shadows create bands of light. You move through the stripes and the gnat clouds. "I can bring you to the ward. I can make something to carry you. On my back."

You look at me. Truly see me. You know it isn't possible. You gaze into my cloudy eye. Your face is streaked with tears. You lean into my body. You grab me and hold me as I have held you.

And then you scream. I feel the scream, hot on my skin, vibrating against my chest. Your ribs heave. Your grief is a turbine, creating more grief.

The forest seems to spin around us, bands of wavering light.

This is how we pass the night. The fighter engines tearing across the sky. The sound of distant bombings. Flashes that flood the sky.

Then quiet. Then sleep.

And when you wake, it is dawn. The air is thick with smoke that smells metallic. And I am now small. I am now fibrous and leathery, shining with an oiliness like creosote. My skin is a kind of sinuous chrysalis. My eye is hidden.

You still will not believe that I am dead.

I am not dead.

You realize that you can, in fact, fashion something to carry me on your back.

You start hunting for the right limbs and vines to build a carrier with straps that you can put over your shoulders and hold at your chest.

You remember being with Proctor Yelzbin, being a girl hunting hybrids in the woods. How you dismantled them for the go-go-roundies.

But you are no longer the girl you once were. And you never really were Ilsa Kerr. If Roon means mystery, you are a mystery to yourself.

Building the carrier takes time and muscle.

When it is finished, you have to put your back against mine, and, pushing with your boots, you roll me into the kind of vine of netting.

You are thinking: what if there is no mystery. What if we are all killers and property and originals and copies and scavengers and poseys and incubators. We shift between states by changing how we are seen by others. By how we see ourselves. Like a fresh new eye opening up from the skin of a hull where we least expect it.

There is still the droning of propulsion engines over the trees. Some are quick and light.

You squat low, get the weight onto the middle of your back and you stand. I wobble a bit. But you stand firm. I am the weight of a human but condensed into something that one might mistake for a porous rock, almost volcanic. My skin is a leathery organ, weathered and ashen.

For a second, you pause, achieving balance and then you head out of the forest. We jostle along. The sky drifting toward morning.

"It is a new war," you tell me. "We will be hunted by many people. But if the Ward takes us in . . . Maybe we can help them. And they can help us. You will survive and be strong again. We will get out of here. Somehow."

You are created a story for us to move into, and you know it. But it helps.

"I have to see them. I can't go forward without knowing where I came from."

Your legs burn and your shoulders ache. Your palms are scratched up from the rough bark of the homemade straps. The trees start to thin.

And, finally, we step out of the woods into the stalk fields.

Strange creatures buzz in the sky. They have metallic, sturdy bodies with goose-like necks. "What are they?" you ask, knowing I cannot answer.

A few hum overhead and linger. They send out red beams of light that flutter over us.

"They're collecting data. They're Gentry-built and report back to Gentry that we're here. A defective and a loose cacheme."

You let them take us in. You cannot stop now. Your legs feel rubbery. "We're getting closer," you tell me. "The ward will be in sight soon."

But you are suddenly worried that it is gone. Worried that you'll get to the small rise where you should be able to see it, and there will be an empty cavity. Like the ward has been ripped from the horizon leaving behind a huge scar.

"It'll be there," you tell yourself. "Wards don't just disappear."

You fear Proctor Yelzbin was a figment. The cachemes were inventions. Maybe you created love where there wasn't any.

"Maybe this is what happens when you want something too much."

When we get to a rise, the ward comes into view. Everything that had gone ghostly takes form again. A building of barred windows collared by a dirt-packed yard and tall gate.

No go-go-roundies, and only one light shining from a room on the third floor, the quarantined floor, a bright eye lonesomely keeping watch.

"That's my ward."

If I were able I would ask, *Does it feel like home?*

But I know the answer. It does.

You head downhill. Though my body is here, you miss me. With me, you could be big and strong and hidden, at the same time.

As we get close to the tall black fence, you stop. A vine you don't recognize has begun to crawl up as if grafting itself to the metal. The gate door is unlocked. You kick it and walk across the yard. You pause at the three steps to the front door. You know each step, the vibration through your leg bones up into your slatted ribs. You heft me up, push open the door to the small parlor and step inside.

You lower the carrier to the sofa. "This is where they'd come. This is where the Gentry parents would show up. They'd wait for Proctor Yelzbin to do paperwork and call the cachemes down."

The wallpaper, its yellow flowers. You feel sick. You hate this room, this sofa, the flowers.

You want me to recognize the ward from the memories, the ones that coursed from your brain into my body. I want to tell you that I am here. But cannot.

You walk to the doorframe. You wanted to come home, to your people. You hadn't expected so much pain. You walk through the parlor. "Proctor Yelzbin!"

But the air is dead. This home feels gutted, a tongue cut from a mouth.

You lift me to your back again and run down the hall and up the stairs. The barred windows gaze at you.

Barred so the cachemes wouldn't jump.

It was not lovely here.

You run into the boys' dormitory room. The mattresses have been stripped and stacked in a corner. The black creep mold has taken over two walls, working on a third.

The girls' dormitory room smells like the lice shampoo and lemony soaps that I had offered up. And lye and bleach. The mattresses are stripped and piled up here, too.

The metal springs have rusted to a burnt orange.

You move to the third floor, the quarantined room.

Where the light is still on.

But the large open room is empty too.

You are not sure what to do. It is over. You are sure of it. They abandoned you. They are gone.

You turn to leave, but then you see it: in big red letters, there are three words written on the wall: PLAY THE GAME.

"I don't know what it means. Or who it was meant for."

You walk to the wall and touch the letter G. It smears like it is not paint or chalk but written in some kind of mold. "We'd always have to douse the walls to keep the mold at bay." Did someone scrub all but these words so the mold would grow this message? *Play the game.* This is no game. You put your hands on the words, arms wide. You touch your forehead to the wall. They're gone. All of them. Lost forever.

You miss them so fiercely that you are fueled with anger. You drag your fists over the red mold, smearing it like blood. You look at your red hands. "We're not playing a game."

There's a hum in the air. You look out. More long-necks.

You walk out of the room, numb and dazed, down the hall. Proctor Yelzbin's bedroom door stands open. You never were allowed in. You see her dresser, move to it quickly, and start opening drawers. You know what you are looking for—proof that all of the memories are real.

You open the bottom drawer. It is full of braids.

You dig through the silken and puffed braids. You find your own and hold it up for a moment.

She tried to help. She cared for you.

Play the game? Could it be a message?

You don't move or speak. Your mind doesn't drift or float. You forget your body. The burden of me on your back. You forget the braids and the drawer and the room. You see through it all to some white expandable nothingness. That nothingness reaches out from here in all directions. It wraps around my casing.

It flits down the stairs.

And then out and out and out.

The nothingness expands past the stalk field and the hill and into the woods. It folds over the hulls' bodies in the tank fields.

It keeps going. Like sunlight in every direction.

But then it stretches too thin, and it stutters and snaps in on itself.

It snaps so hard that it thunders in your chest.

You see Proctor Yelzbin's face in your mind, held by the metal digging into the soft skin. Sharp and fierce, she leans forward and whispers, "Play the game."

Play the game.

Heat spreads from my chest to yours. I am amorphous and eyeless, but no longer cold. I want you to know I am alive. I want you to keep going.

You only know one game.

The tables cleared out of the basement cafeteria . . . hoops and stars.

We head down to the basement.

Light streams in the high small windows of the cafeteria. You look out one of them. The air outside thrums with long-necks, and, in the distance, fighters and two-man pods, manned by Gentry. A Gentry pod homes in on the ward and circles the yard. Did we lead the long-necks here and the pods followed?

The tanks and terrariums that used to sit on the window ledges are gone, and so are the bittlefish and the eye-lings that would drag their damp wings from cocoons to air them before flight. Your arms have grown weak. You lay me on a table.

You push back tables and lift benches, revealing the lines and circles on the floor.

"Hoops and stars," you explain. "The starter would throw three balls to the others. There were goal markers." At either end of the cafeteria, shoulder-height boxes are painted onto the walls.

You search for the balls but the bin in the corner is empty. "They're gone," I say. "I'll pretend. I'll show you how it goes."

You position yourself as the starter, moving to the black center circle which sits in another blue circle within an oval.

"It's like an eye," you explain to me. "That's what Proctor Yelzbin would say. *Go stand in the eye. Back to the eye, the pupil.*"

You stand on the black circle, the pupil, but the floor is unsteady. It wobbles under your feet. It is loose.

"It's not an eye anymore," you say. "It's a door."

Darkness. A pupil, yes. A dilated pupil. But also a hole that will take you away from me. In this moment, I am certain. These are your people, your past. This is what you've wanted—to go home.

But you carry me with you. You reposition my body in the carrier on your back, walk down the ladder and close the circular door behind us.

A faint light shines at the end of a long dirt tunnel. It turns.

When you hoist me up a little, I conform to your back. I grow and wrap small appendages around your shoulders, starting to support my own weight. I am still formless, but it gives you another bit of hope.

Grazing the wall with one hand, you move toward a door. You hear noises on the other side—voices, clattering . . . You open the door.

It swings wide.

A room filled with ten horse-hybrids, still and silent, power-down. Shining eyes and manes and hoofs. Thick healthy coats of fur, muzzles and tails. The air smells musty and burnt. Beyond the hybrids, a few young cachemes sit against a wall. Some doze. Others watch us, warily. You don't recognize any of them.

Except one. "EOtt."

She turns to face you. "Roon? Why are you here? You shouldn't be here. It's not safe."

She hugs you, and you know that she was important to you. "Tell me, EOtt. Tell me what's happening?"

"The proctors weren't making go-go-roundies to sell," EOtt explains. "The go-go-roundies were just a cover. They wanted hybrids to hide the cachemes in and take them to safety. Things aren't good up there, are they?"

"Not good at all." You look at the chachemes. "Where are the cachemes that were here when I left?"

"Yelzbin got our own out first. These are sent from other wards who heard what she's doing." EOtt opens a compartment under the hybrid's ribs. "See all the supplies?" she says. "The children climb up inside. It's small and tight but it has water and food rations."

EOtt shuts the compartment and moves to the hybrid's head. "We'll go out like a lost herd. No one cares about out-moded hybrids anymore. The cachemes will be safely stored inside." EOtt looks at all of the cachemes. "This is the last group. Yelzbin and I will go out with them."

"Where is she?"

"She'll be happy to see you," EOtt says. "You were her favorite."

EOtt points to a room down another hallway, not far. A small, dark space. Proctor Yelzbin is standing over a desk, writing notes on a hand-drawn map. You barely recognize her. Her uniform is wrinkled and dirty. She wears no headdress, no sleeping hood. Her brow is stitched.

You walk over and touch her arm. She startles and turns.

Her eyes dart over your face. She doesn't say anything. She just gazes. She drinks you in. And you can't quite process that she is real. Her dainty chin, the sharp bridge of her nose, the squint of her dark eyes and soft smile.

"They shunted my memories but they came back," you tell Proctor Yelzbin. "I saw your face. I remembered you."

Proctor Yelzbin's eyes are weary, but they shine with tears. "I was notified that you were being transported. But you escaped?"

You turn so she can see me in the carrier. "Yes, with the hull, and they offered scents and once I started to remember, it came rushing back."

Proctor Yelzbin smiles.

"I wish you could see them in their full form. They're—" You are about to cry. I am your hull, and you are my wick. How to explain that? "They protected me. We survived because of each other. And I remember so much of my past now."

"How much? Everything?" Proctor Yelzbin says.

"Not everything, no."

"I whispered it to you just once."

"What did you whisper to me?"

"The story of a man whose wife died."

"I don't know this story. Tell me again."

"The man mourned his wife. And, in his grief, he turned to the comforts of a posey girl. But he didn't just turn to *any* posey girl." Her eyes are pinched and teary. You don't understand. "He went looking for the cacheme of his young dead wife. That was who he missed. That was who he wanted back."

Your chest tightens. You feel flushed.

"He found her. And he paid for her. And he made her turn her face away from him so he didn't see her marking scar. Only the smooth side of her face."

You are starting to understand. You draw in a breath then your throat seizes. "You know this," you whisper, "you know this because you were that posey girl." How else could she know? Why else would she have been so scared for girls being repurposed? This is why she cut your hair so short, why she has a drawer full of braids.

Proctor Yelzbin unbuttons her collar and pulls her shirt off her shoulder. A dark line runs across the meat of her upper arm. "This is the mark for each birth of an incubator. I was being transferred from posey girl to incubator. My anatomy had been altered for this new position. It was a window of time and you were made within me," she says. "When I told him, he arranged for me to move with you, into the ward. To raise you as a proctor. It was a kindness."

"Who is Ilsa Kerr?"

"There is no Ilsa Kerr."

"I was your incubator, your proctor."

"*My mother.*" You reach out and touch Proctor Yelzbin's face. "I was your mystery, your roon."

"*Mo rún,*" Proctor Yelzbin says. "Not my mystery. My *secret.*" She pulls you to her chest. As she holds you, she whispers, "Come with us. Come with us."

You close your eyes. You hold your breath and nod; the wooliness of her dress is rough against your cheek. As you smell the wool and the faint imprint of soldered wires, you think this is the smell of mother and love.

"We will take care of you." She pulls back and looks at you. "And get you to freedom."

"My hull can help. They will grow large and strong again. They will be helpful. They can help get us out of here. Far away."

"Your hull can't come with us. They'll be looking for them—both sides. Gentry because the hull has gone rogue and revolutionaries because the hull is a threat. You need to let them go. They're a target. They'll get you killed. Leave them. Come with us. We can keep you safe."

Your heart is wild. I feel it drumming. I am suspended in time. I barely exist. I wait. Time stretches. It seems like I can hear distant thunder, and I have to wait for the storm. And I am certain that this storm will be a kind of sadness I've never known before. But then you say, "I can't. I can't come with you. The hull and I are bound."

As soon as you say it, it is the truth. It is real. We might make it. We might not. But we'll be together. You know what you want—you know it on the surface of your tingling skin, within your trembling hands and deep inside of your chest, your heart beating hard and fast as the kind of bird I once explained to your—a bird made of memory. You will not let me go.

Above ground, gunshots.

"I have to go," you say.

"We have to move quickly here, too." She hugs you one last time. "You're always with me."

"And you are always with me."

You carry me, running out of the ward, beyond the gate. We are heading back uphill toward the cover of scrub-trees. I am wrapped around your back now, holding on, warm and steady, very much alive. You release the carrier straps and let it fall, knowing I am holding tight.

I have enough energy to open one of my eyes. Battles have overtaken the sky. A squadron of long-necks moves in a tightening radius. Three pods fly in close then lift. They open fire on each other. Exploding and careening and thudding into the ground.

We are trapped in a war. For us, it doesn't matter who is winning and who is losing. We will suffer either way.

I find my voice. *Roon, thank you. For choosing me.*

You fall to the ground. I tumble off of your back. I am in a small and wobbly form. But I grow hoofs. I stagger to stand. With my one eye, we stare at each other. "You are still with me."

I never left you.

"I didn't choose you," you tell me. "We chose each other." You seem charged, as if your chest is full of electric thistles.

A pod buzzes so close that we feel the vibrations in our bones. We take off running. I am at your heels. We run as fast as we can.

Then you stumble, catch yourself, and look up. "Why is the sky turning?"

The clouds are twisting into a strange grayish silver.

The long-necks turn mad circles. The Gentry pods hover. Their engines whine, and then they're gone. The revolutionaries' fighter vessels figure out they're in trouble, too, and they take off.

For a moment, everything gets strangely quiet and still. "What's coming?"

I don't know.

You turn to see the Ward. Through the thick smoke, the hybrids have started their trek in the opposite direction. Hiding inside of them are the cachemes, EOtt, and Proctor Yelzbin.

The hybrids look up at the sky too. It shimmers translucent, almost silky.

Not far off, racing toward the hybrids, is a billowing cloud of chaff-eaters. They rise and dip then seem to stall, suddenly hesitant.

The silvery air thickens.

"We need cover!" you shout.

We run toward the scrub trees.

The air contracts. It is pulled from our lungs. It spins up from the scrub trees, the grass, and the dirt itself. The air is drawn into the sky, an invisible funnel, and, suddenly, we're caught in it, lifted off our feet.

My skin is slick with condensation. The wind is fierce. It whips around us.

The sky convulses, and we're thrown forward. We land hard on the ground. It, too, is wet as if covered in dew.

The ward shimmers for a moment like it is reflected in glass. And then, as if winking, the light on the third floor goes out. The windows shatter against their bars. The roof tiles peel loose and spray upward. The shed pops off its foundation and skitters, smashing into the far gate. Toys, wheelers, and tools kick across the yard. The whole building sways, drunkenly, spins a quarter turn, curtseys, then collapses.

The chaff-eaters are swept up, churning within it.

The dust and debris whirl, as if the sky were starving.

You try to track the hybrids in the fuming destruction. They're lifted and spinning. You lose track of them.

And then, finally, the air pinches. The swarm of chaff eaters rises and falls, creating a veil that's hard to see through.

You reach out and pull me close. You are worried. Is your mother dead? EOtt and the cachemes?

"Where are they?"

You feel fragile and rent open. As if you are made of nothing more than a handful of eyelings, and the small butterflies are dragging themselves from cocoons and abandoning your broken chest, nothing more than a cavity. Holding loss.

We lie side by side. You turn toward me. I want to comfort you but there is little comfort I can offer. *I am sorry.*

You look up at the sky, breathing hard. You scream. It is long and loud.

And as if it is felt by the air around us, the sky's silver pales to a bleached white.

"Is another blast coming?"

We have to leave this place.

"How?"

A disoriented fighter vessel cuts through the thick air. The pilot's head bobbles. The windshield is cracked. The pilot is dead. The vessel is rogue. Its pattern makes no sense. We scramble to a rock that juts out of the hill. We huddle there.

Its landing gear has been engaged. When it comes close, we can reach for it. It might fly far from here before it crashes.

"Are you sure you can do it?"

My body swells a bit. I grow taller and broader. My skin is now oily, ready for more change. I engage an internal lightness. A reorganization of muscles in my legs. An ability to leap. To propel myself. *Yes.*

"Once we're up there, we can climb into the water-landing gear—they're fat gliders, carved-out like canoes."

It is only a few seconds before the vessel is swerving near the rock. The air clouded by debris.

You shout over the roaring engine, "Ready?"

Yes.

As the vessel dips close, we reach up and grab hold. Our bodies jerk forward.

We are airborne. Your boots kick wildly to keep from twisting. The wind tears at us. We hoist ourselves onto the water-landing gear. Wind-battered, we cower in the small well.

We look over the edge, the wind in our faces.

You look for the hybrids and see them moving like the crooked backbone of a giant hull. They are making their way.

The vessel turns, and you can no longer see them, but you know that they're alive and this gives you hope.

When they shunted your memory, they didn't understand that memory begins on the surface of the senses, the bristle of nerve-endings, the repetitive jitter of muscles, the swell of a chest, the tilt of light, the taste and scent of existence, and it drills into a moment, drills you into the ground, into your essence. It becomes the invisible bulwark that keeps us tied to each other. It can't be snipped away. It burrows and creates a home within us.

And it happens every moment. It never stops.

We crest the wooded hill, fly over woods. We see the Wasted Plains below, littered with dead hulls. Cargo planes are hauling their bodies away.

We're racing over dirt and rough shrubs and bowing grasses. You tear your eyes away from the ground below. You put your hand on my claw. The wind is strong

You draw images to the surface of your mind:

The bright pollen as we cut across the green fields.

Proctor Yelzbin with seed puffs dotting her hair. As a posey girl, young and scared.

The drawer full of braids.

The smell when you hugged her, a collective scent pocketed in the dip of her neck.

Warmth radiates from my skin to yours.

The vessel is rushing away from the woods and the ward in a direction we've never gone before.

You imagine another world, like the woods below, but free from fear. You imagine Proctor Yelzbin and EOtt there, blinking into the new light glinting through the new trees. And in that version of the woods, we are with them, but we are not yet fully etched. Like the opposite of a ghost that lingers behind, we are a shape that lingers in the future, waiting to be filled in.

The northern horizon is blurred by plumes of thick smoke. Heading south, we fly over desiccated land splotched, here and there, with oil slicks and dead factories. Occasionally, a spray of sun-bleached ruins—skeletal buildings and outposts like the gear-and-spoke remains of hybrids picked bare.

Our bodies are being rattled so hard that everything seems flimsy. Even the bones of the world seem frail and brittle. The wind whips away the old ash and chrysalis of my exterior. My skin feels slack, as if he's poised to grow.

And then I do.

The vessel jags sharply to the side.

Get in.

You scramble in quickly.

The vessel dips into a death spiral.

Our heads are airy and doused with light, sun-struck. It is as if we're caught in a glowing mist, a radiant haze, as if being polished by millions of tiny bright, flaring embers. Is this the moment just before our bodies turn to ash and ghost up into air like a fogged collective breath?

I sense the ending, a release. We're going to be snuffed out. A thin trail of smoke.

Our hearts flutter against each other. I no longer know which beats belong to whom.

We spin.

Ready?

I feel your body coil. Mine does too. And then we spring forward, in unison. We leap.

We are in a field. A tremor of air. A breeze, yes. And light that shivers.

We have landed again but this time it is different. We are each our own, but I am of you. You are of me.

Are we safe? No. Not really. Not ever. That is not what our existence has offered us.

We are healing each other. We are creating our past, weaving it and reweaving it as we move in and out of wakefulness. It has been strange, the making. We have been aware of it and not. We have been fashioning it with something like touch, something like pressing and molding. But it has felt like trudging among reeds to collect things—eyelings, pale fronds, and live frogs with their puffed throats gone taut, shiny and thin.

We are collecting, but it is still something made. Or else it wouldn't truly exist. Made for each other.

It is not my voice moving to your skin. There is no barrier between us now. The story shifts between us, as if with currents and tides.

What we are making is like a bud, tight and compressed. A bud that holds a small galaxy with pollen that can spin out like stars.

We stitch the journey from space elevator to land. We suspend time in the Hellwash Mounds and, later, running through the green fields. We circle the fallen soldier in the field and we move around the Grip and through the herd in the Wasted Plains.

My near death is now ours. Your mother is now ours. This thing that we have made is proof that we are not simply what they made us for. We are our own beings. And our past exists in some space, some unknowable, untouchable place.

It is ours. It is all true, but not the truth. Not one truth. Many truths, a blur of them. This makes a fuller truth.

It remains. The way scents can punch holes in memory, the holes will remain—like holes of light. Holes we can put an eye up to. And the view will expand and contract.

It is a new kind of roon—a poem, an incantation, a spell, a mystery unwound, a secret whispered, murmured, roared . . .

Ours. We can be distinct and we can be one. For now, we are whole.

It starts as we started: *We are in a stall. We are in a glass box. Our horns grow and recede. A black flower blooms in one of our eyes.*

ACKNOWLEDGMENTS

This story has lived many lives. I'm thankful to all the people who helped along the way, especially Justin Manask, Dave Scott, Matt Bondurant, Ann VanderMeer, Mark Teppo, Darin Bradley, and Brendan Deneen. And I'm so grateful to my family, including our Fray-Fray.